TRULY YOURS

DARA GIRARD

ILORI
Press Books, LLC

ISBN: 978-1949764000

TRULY YOURS

Printed in the United States of America

Cover photo © Katy Duclos/Unsplash

This is a work of fiction. Names, characters, places and incidents are either the product of the author's imagination or are used fictitiously, and any resemblance to actual persons, living or dead is entirely coincidental.

ILORI PRESS BOOKS, LLC

P.O. Box 10332

Silver Spring, MD 20914

www.iloripressbooks.com

Table for Two

Gaining Interest

Careless Rapture

Dangerous Curves

Familiar Stranger

It Happened One Wedding

Unexpected Pleasure

Midnight Promise

Sweet Temptation

Always and Forever

Clifton Sisters

The Sapphire Pendant

The Amber Stone

The Emerald Ring

Fortune Brothers

A Tempting Proposal

A Seductive Arrangement

Novels

Honest Betrayal

The Daughters of Winston Barnett

Remember My Name

Illusive Flame

Winterwood Lane

DEAR READER LETTER

Dear Reader,

Welcome to the fifth book in the *It Happened One Wedding* series where the best part of the story comes after "I do."

Nice guys.

A lot of nice guys get overlooked for the heartbreakers, players, and downright jerks. Why? Lots of reasons, but one is that they can easily be taken for granted (nice girls too but that's another story!).

I wondered, *What would happen if a nice guy got fed up being 'the best friend' and set out to change himself?*

So I added a bet between cousins, a sassy ER doctor and a kitten with attitude and came up with the book you now have.

I hope you enjoy Trent and Erin's story in *Truly Yours*.

All the best,

Dara

You can find out more about this series and learn about my other titles on my website www.daragirard.com

CHAPTER 1

"You shouldn't have come. You're only torturing yourself."

Trent Brewster rubbed his chin, keeping his gaze straight ahead as the sun seeped through the stain glass windows of the church casting swaths of red, yellow and blue on the wooden choir benches. Five large bouquets of white and red roses scented the air, as he listened to the rustling of starched shirts and flowing dresses, people sniffing into tissues, kids shifting in seats and low giggles from two boys in the back pew followed by a harsh 'shhh' sound. He knew his cousin was right. He should have stayed away. But the torture felt good. It reminded him that he was still alive although when Dorothy had told him she was getting married he'd felt like he was dying.

Still did if he was honest with himself.

He felt a sharp elbow in the ribs and winced. He shot his cousin a look.

She met his gaze. "I mean it."

"Shut up," he warned her, casting a nervous look at the sea of colorful hats that surrounded them. They sat in the middle pew of the sparsely tended section reserved for the bride's family and friends. The grooms' side seemed to be bursting with people. They were packed so tight into the pews that twice he'd seen a young boy shoved into the aisle before he scrambled back into his seat, squeezing himself next to a thin man who seemed to be half asleep. The man's head kept bobbing forward before jerking up at different times.

In comparison, Trent had an arm's length distant between him and the expensively dressed woman in the yellow and green stripped pinwheel hat and matching shoes to his right. So he didn't really need to be worried about someone overhearing his cousin above the deep, powerful sound of the flamboyant pastor who couldn't seem to say a full statement without punctuating it with a "Hallelujah!" and shooting his hand in the air like a spring coil.

But that didn't matter. He didn't want to talk. He wanted to suffer. In silence.

She jabbed him with her elbow again. This time hard enough to make him jerk and grunt.

People turned to him, curious.

He cleared his throat, feeling heat rising up his neck. "Sorry."

The woman in the pinwheel hat flashed a bright smile at him. "No, brother, don't be ashamed," she said in a sweet island lilt. "Let the spirit move you."

Trent plastered on a smile in return as he heard his

cousin stifle a giggle. He turned to her, half wanting to rip off the pretty pink hat she wore on her head and toss it like a Frisbee. She blinked her big, brown eyes unapologetic. Her eyes were her nicest feature. She'd inherited the haughty Brewster chin and angular jaw giving her an arrogant look. He lowered his voice. "What is wrong with you? Stop hitting me."

"I will when you stop looking like that."

"Like what?"

"Like your heart's being torn in two. Cut it out."

He sighed. He didn't care what he looked like. He only needed to get through the ceremony—the everlasting, torturous ceremony—in one piece.

Trent forced himself to let his gaze rest on the beaming, beautiful bride as she gazed at the man to whom she was willing to pledge her life. To share her life. He saw the lovely glow of her cocoa cheeks, her soft red lips, the luscious curves of her body. He knew how it felt to have her smile at him; the touch of her soft, warm lips against his; the feel of her fingers on his body. And now she belonged to someone else—forever. Not him.

Never him.

He swallowed, tasting the crumbs of pain and bitterness.

Dorothy Carlson wasn't the first woman to spurn his love. But she would be the last. This wedding was the torture he needed to remind himself that love wasn't for him. His loyalty. His devotion. His love was never enough. He'd forever be relegated into the dreaded "friend-zone".

Women didn't want the nice guy, the good guy, the

dependable guy. They wanted men like Derrick Ellis who'd ignored Dorothy for five months before he asked her out. A man who'd twice forgotten days that were important to her—her birthday and her father's passing.

"It doesn't matter Trent," Dorothy had once told him. "When he did remember my birthday, he made up for it." Then, to his horror and disgust, she'd told him every detail of what Derrick had done, treating him like the asexual ex-boyfriend she though he was. If he could have scrubbed his brain of the memory he would have.

No, Dorothy loved Derrick. Not Trent. Not the guy who had remembered every birthday, anniversary and memorial remembrance over the two years they'd dated. The guy who had held her when her beloved grandfather died. The guy who had helped throw a surprise party for her thirtieth birthday.

For two years he'd felt as if he'd finally met the woman to spend his life with. He knew after four months but didn't want to rush it. He'd hinted about marriage after eight, but she always changed the subject and he didn't want to pressure her. He never wanted to force her and thought she would come around. That she'd soon discover that she felt the same way about him as he did her. That they were perfect together.

But he'd been blind. Dorothy hadn't felt the same. Trent still remembered the tears swimming in her eyes when she told him it wasn't working. That she loved him but not in *that* way. "Can't we stay friends?"

He should have said no. He should have walked away and never spoken to her again. But he didn't move. He didn't move for what seemed like hours as he lay in his bed, listening to the hammering of his heart. He'd thought the night had been perfect. She wasn't supposed to be saying this. He must have misunderstood. He started to laugh. That was it. He'd misheard her.

Dorothy sniffed. "Why are you laughing?"

"I thought I heard you say you wanted to be friends."

"I do."

His heart hammered louder. He still didn't move. "Did you know this before or after you slept with me?"

"Don't make this harder than it is."

He sat up in the bed and stared at her amazed. "Harder? Who breaks up with someone right after sex? At least pretend you liked it."

She gathered the sheets to cover her chest and lowered her gaze. "I did like it." She met his eyes, beseeching him to understand. "I always like it. You know that."

He rested his head against the headboard. "I don't understand."

"It's not about sex."

Of course it was about sex. She was telling him he wasn't good enough. "Couldn't you have waited until morning? Or told me before?"

"It's not you." She rested a hand on his chest. "You're a great—"

He moved away. Her gentle touch felt like a slap. "Lay?"

"I was going to say 'guy'."

"Don't insult me."

"I'm not. I don't want you to think—"

This was all wrong. He'd been so happy only minutes

before. How had this happened? When? Why? "Feelings like this don't come out of nowhere. Why did you come over tonight if you knew—?"

"I didn't know. I thought if we were together I'd feel different. You're a lot of fun." She lowered her voice and her gaze, looking sad. "And I love you...just not in that way. You're a wonderful—"

And she kept talking, but he didn't care about the words. None of it mattered. Nothing mattered. She could give a three hour lecture on all his good points, all he heard was *I don't love you. I never loved you. I never will love you.* Trent wanted to close his eyes and cover his ears and shout, "Stop, stop, stop. You're hurting me. You're hurting me. Why don't you love me?!" But he stayed still. If he didn't move, he could pretend it wasn't happening.

She wiped away her tears. "And this is hard for me—"

There was that damn word again. Hard. Yes, he'd been hard for her only a few hours, complimenting her on the sexy summer dress she'd shown up in. She'd smiled and told him it was new. (Had the smile been real?) He remembered the sound her dress made as he slowly slid it off her body; the soft gasps from her lips as he made love to her. (Had that been fake too?) He'd imagined every night like this. The rest of their lives. Now he felt like he'd been gutted.

"I don't want to lose you. I know it will be hard—"

He gritted his teeth. "Difficult."

"What?"

Stop using the word "hard". "Just say it will be difficult."

"Okay...it will be difficult at first and awkward, but

you're important to me and I want to keep our special relationship somehow. Losing my dad was one of the biggest losses in my life. I don't think I could bear losing you too. Please tell me we can still be friends. Maybe not now, but someday."

And he'd said yes. Stupid as it was. Painful as it was. He'd said yes. All because he was a good guy who hated to see her cry. It didn't matter that he wanted to cry too. That he wanted to understand why she didn't love him. Why couldn't it be him?

Dorothy had been the fourth woman to let him down easy. Thankfully, the only one to break up with him post-coitus, he never wanted that to happen again. He'd make sure. The moment a woman started crying in bed he was getting out of there. At least he'd learned that lesson.

His "Can't we be friends?" streak started in senior year of high school. She was in the drama club; he'd been part of the stage crew. They'd hit if off immediately. He didn't even see the possible breakup coming and it hit him like a tuba. She wanted to "stay in touch" and "remain friends". He nodded mutely, inwardly glad he wouldn't see her again—they were going to different universities—determined he'd get over her and start anew. He had a disastrous rebound relationship with another woman, a theater major, who shoved him into the friend-zone after six months telling him he was "so sweet".

He wondered if she'd still think him sweet if he threw up on her shoes. What guy wants to be called "sweet"? But he smiled and accepted the breakup and the intermittent phone calls and messages she'd send him when she broke up with someone who "shattered her heart".

He didn't date for the next several years. He wanted to be a success. Girls liked successful guys, right? Successful guys didn't end up in the friend-zone. So he focused on his schooling, studied engineering, joined a major acoustics design firm and began dating Carlene.

He thought she liked him. She said he was perfect. He said the same.

Then she told him they were too perfect together and she was bored.

She found someone more exciting. An accountant. An accountant named Harold. Really? *He* was more boring than an accountant who worked in his father's business? Yes, she told him, because he surprises me and makes me laugh. "But I'd still love to be friends," were her parting words.

Fortunately, she moved to Ecuador and they lost touch—although every once in a while she still sent him a text or email. He deleted them. Especially the ones showing her kids—two cute girls.

And now Dorothy. Dorothy had been the worst. Dorothy had hurt him more than all the rest because by thirty-three he thought he'd gotten women all figured out. He didn't cling, he didn't pressure. He encouraged her in her career. He told her she was beautiful. He tried to make her feel special. He surprised her and tried to keep the relationship interesting.

But it hadn't been enough.

"You're too good for me, Trent," she'd once told him seven months after their breakup. By that time he'd given up on winning her back and had permanently parked his heart and ego in the dreaded friend-zone.

I don't understand, he wanted to tell her. *I never understand.* But he nodded. He let her go. And they stayed friends because that's what she wanted and he didn't want to hurt her. Although he hurt every day. Even a year later. He thought his feelings would have ebbed, but they were raw and piercing as he saw all the differences between himself and Derrick.

Dr. Derrick Ellis. A Jamaican-American oncologist. Six foot two, dark skinned, rich.

Trent, on the other hand, was just shy of six foot; he thought of himself as more American than Jamaican most times and he made good money but not enough to own a cherry red Ferrari and silver Jag. He shifted his gaze to Dorothy. Had she ever looked at him like that? No. She hadn't. No woman had. No woman would. He knew that now. He accepted it. He would remember this pain. Always. He wouldn't be a fool again.

Trent sensed Mindy move and shifted out of the way before she could poke him again. He knew what he must look like. He'd been told he wore his emotions on his face, but he was beyond caring. No one was paying attention to him. He was just another face in the crowd.

Nobody special. And he'd never seek anyone special again.

They all stood and cheered when the ceremony ended and applauded as the couple came down the aisle. Dorothy caught his eye and stopped. "I'm so glad you came," she whispered, then startled him by leaning forward and kissing him on the cheek, enveloping him in the scent of violets before she walked away.

"Bitch," Mindy mumbled as the couple left the church.

Trent turned sharply to her, but her face was so composed that, for a moment, he thought he'd imagined it. She looped her arm through his. "Come on. Let's go."

CHAPTER 2

In the car, Trent turned on his GPS and scrolled through the screen. "Did you call her a bitch?"

"Yes," Mindy admitted with a shrug. "Why?"

"Wanted to make sure I heard you correctly."

"You sent a RSVP. Of course she knew you were coming. Why is she acting touched and surprised?"

"She's been polite."

"She's being a—Hey!" she cried when Trent pulled her hat down over her face.

He looked back at the map on the screen.

Mindy checked her hat for any possible damage then put it back on her head, adjusting it just so before she frowned at the map on the screen. "What are you doing?"

"I programmed the car to take us to the reception. I'm making sure I—"

She stared at him alarmed then hit him in the arm. "You idiot."

He turned to her wide-eyed. "What now?"

"You're going to the reception too?" She gestured to the white church looming large under a blue summer sky. "Wasn't this enough?"

No. He wanted more. Let him see her happy. Happy with someone else. A trial by fire.

I said I'd come. "I heard the food will be good."

Mindy covered her face and let out a tiny squeal of frustration. "I hate her!"

"You don't mean that."

She sighed and stared at him. "You don't know anything." She shook her head; when she spoke her voice sounded sad. "I love you but you're clueless. The only reason I'm here is because...I didn't want you to come alone. But you should have taken my advice."

With the GPS set Trent sat back and started the ignition. "Your advice sounded childish."

"It's not childish to get a little revenge. What was wrong with letting me set you up with my gorgeous friend, Rachelle, and pretending that she's your girlfriend?"

"Dorothy wouldn't care."

"Doesn't matter. At least you'd look like you were over her. Instead you drag your cousin along as your date to your ex-girlfriend's wedding. Do you know how pathetic that looks?"

Trent turned to her, his voice hard. "Yes, I do know. Because I'm pathetic, right? And you think she wouldn't have seen right through me if I brought Rachelle here and fawned all over her? Does that even sound like me? I know what you and every other woman think of me. I know why I'm the 'friend'. I've been in the friend-zone long enough to know that I'm parked there permanently." He shook his head. "No, that's wrong. I'm not parked. I'm fastened with cement and bolted by chains. I couldn't move if I wanted to."

His cousin sighed with regret. "I didn't mean to say—"

"Yes, you did and you're right. I know what people think of me. If my family hasn't taught me, life certainly has."

"Don't bring them up right now."

She was right. The thought of his family was too depressing. She was one of the few relatives he could stomach. The rest drove him mad.

"She wasn't the one," Mindy said. "It's as simple as that. There is someone out there who—"

Trent shook his head. "BS. And I'm done with BS. Women say one thing and mean another."

"Not all women."

"No, but enough to let me know that my chances are slim. I'm done. Maybe in ten years I'll try again, but not now. I've learned my lesson. I can't read women. I don't understand them. At least not the ones I'm attracted to. I don't know what they want."

"That's not true."

He nodded and a cynical grin crossed his lips. "You're right. I *do* know what they want. They want someone who's the exact opposite of me."

"Trent. That's not—"

"Yes, it is." He laughed without humor. "It took six months for Dorothy to find her husband. I bet you if I acted different I could find a woman who would want to be exclusive within a month, tell me she loved me two months later and would marry me in six."

Mindy fell quiet for a moment then said, "Prove it."

"What?"

"Prove to me that your theory is right."

"I don't have to prove it. I know it."

"Not every woman wants a man like Uncle Steven."

Trent's cynical grin turned a little cruel. His father had had three wives and numerous girlfriends. Trent couldn't even get one down the aisle. His father had first walked down the aisle at twenty-three. Trent had foolishly thought that by being his father's opposite, not causing the pain his father had, he'd have the family life he craved. He'd desperately wanted a life different than the one he'd grown up in, certain he'd find a woman who'd help him build it. He'd been naïve.

"You haven't met the right woman yet."

He shook his head. Dorothy had been the one. He'd loved her more than he had anyone else. He wouldn't love like that again. Ever. "How about Xavier?"

Mindy shivered as if someone had poured ice water down her back. "He's not a good example."

"He's the perfect example." His brother had the good sense not to marry the women he went through (He'd learned from their father's mistakes), but if he snapped his fingers, he could get a queue lined up of eager women of every age, race and ethnicity ready to take him down the aisle. Trent had watched his older half-brother in action and knew all the moves.

"He's still not married."

"He could be if he wanted to."

"It's still all just a theory. I don't think that by pretending to be like your brother or Uncle Steven you'd be engaged in six months."

Trent shrugged. "I know I'm right. I've never had a woman want to be exclusive with me in under three months. I bet if I acted like Xavier I could get a woman tied to me within a month."

"Willing to bet on it?"

"What are you offering?"

Mindy thought for a moment then said, "If you win I'll donate a thousand dollars to Vince's summer school program that you're always talking about."

He nodded. He had worked with his friend to develop the program. It was Trent's passion to discover different ways to teach people of various ages and abilities the power of mathematics through sound engineering. He held out his hand. "It's a deal."

Mindy waved her hand. "But if you lose, you'll have to let me set you up on five different dates."

"Five?"

"Yes." She grinned. "Are you sure you want to do this? You should be worried. I already have someone in mind."

"I'm not worried." He flashed her a grin in return. "I won't lose. In four weeks I'll have a girlfriend who adores me."

CHAPTER 3

It had been a mistake. A terrible, awful mistake. Asking Jeremiah Attoh to be her wedding date had been one of the worst decisions she'd made in a while.

Fortunately, she was the only one who thought so.

"You are so lucky. I envy you. Where did you pick him up?" Erin's cousin, Caitlin, said with a playful nudge as she eyed Jeremiah from across the reception hall where he laughed with her father. He had the looks of an actor —leading man of course, the one who always got the woman in the end—and the charm of a con man.

"We've been casually seeing each other for a while," Erin said, which was a lie. There was nothing casual about their relationship. It had been very calculating, on both sides. He thought she had connections and she knew she needed to bring someone like him to the wedding to stop her family from wondering about her love life.

"He's gorgeous."

And knows it. "Hmm."

"And smart."

Yes, he's told me that too. "Hmm."

"What company does his father own?"

Erin rattled off the name and heard her cousin sigh. "Your mum will be in heaven."

While I wallow in hell because I didn't want to attend this wedding alone. So she'd ignored her instincts and chosen Jeremiah. It wasn't that she had terrible taste in men. It was that the men she was interested in were never interested in her. They were either scared off by her career (She got a rush out of being an ER doctor working in a small Maryland hospital, the noise, the people, the controlled chaos)the fact that she rode a motorcycle and had built it. Or—as one date had told her —that she had the looks of a woman who could break a man's balls and wear them as earrings. Whatever that meant.

She tried her best to make people feel comfortable around her. She was a great team player, at least her team at the hospital thought so, and she got along with most people at work. It was in her personal life where things seemed to fall apart.

Although her mother said she was sometimes too blunt, too smart and too driven. All were likely true, so she was willing to try to adjust. Which was why she'd gone against her basic nature—a desire for self-preservation—and dated a man like Jeremiah. A man who spent most of the time talking about himself.

She didn't mind. She didn't have much to say. She

didn't talk about work. She usually lied about being a doctor in public, because when they did find out then people opened up about intimate problems they thought she might be able to help them with.

This was normal. She had to act normal. She wasn't supposed to be bored. Women were supposed to like weddings and receptions, right? They were supposed to like wearing pretty dresses and sipping champagne. And maybe she would, if she didn't feel like a show horse, prancing around trying to show off her assets. Unfortunately, according to her mother, she'd gotten that wrong too. "How could you wear black to your cousin's wedding?!" she'd shrieked when she'd seen Erin's dress.

"It's not black it's dark green."

"You wear green scrubs at work, couldn't you have selected a different color? You should have let me come with you."

"Thanks Mum. But I think I'm finally old enough to dress myself."

Her mother kissed her teeth. "Don't be facety."

It was the only way to survive the constant feeling of falling short of their expectations. But that was what was expected, right? That was also normal. Lots of women felt this way. Although she expected few other women had bought the same dress four times in the same shade. She didn't like going to the dry cleaners and didn't care about being seen in the same outfit, so if this dress got too sweaty she had an easy replacement for another night out. But that was neither here nor there.

Tonight she promised she'd be normal. She wouldn't imagine various grisly scenarios like she usually did.

She wouldn't imagine what she would do if the large cake knife slipped while the bride and groom cut the cake and sliced through a major nerve (missing an artery, she didn't want too much blood) of the bride's hand, or wonder how to proceed if the fan's propeller, above them, fell and cut someone's neck, not a complete decapitation, but close, she'd read a story where a young boy had survived. Or perhaps, if someone collapsed suffering from irregular breathing. She'd rush to the rescue. She'd be useful.

She loved helping people.

When she wasn't helping, she felt useless. Like right now. Her cousin was complimenting her on something that had nothing to do with her. Nothing to do with anything important. But it made her family happy and wanting to see your family happy was normal. Tonight she'd mimic Dorothy, her cousin Derrick's blushing bride (well not exactly blushing she looked triumphant, well aware of the catch she'd attained. Erin wouldn't be surprised if Dorothy had a slight mean streak, but so did her cousin so they'd be well matched). She looked like she'd be a great addition to the family as her aunt liked to tell everyone. She owned a lucrative design firm.

There was nothing lucrative about Erin's career, yet. Her father was disappointed she wasn't a proper doctor. He'd read about the possible income of other specialties and the amount of burnout ER doctor's suffered. "You're a little too intense sometimes, my love," her father liked to tell her. He always added "my love" when he offered criticism. "You should consider opening your own practice."

But she didn't want her own practice. She wanted to keep doing what she loved for as long as she could.

Her family likely wouldn't worry about her love life as much if she'd chosen a career path they'd deemed more suitable. As it stood they found her disappointing on two fronts. Her family loved her but worried. Worried that she'd be burnout and alone forever. An immigrant parent's nightmare.

Tonight she'd give them nothing to worry about.

"You should go dance with him," Caitlin said. "You make a great couple. You look so good together."

She'd slept with him once—another mistake—and still couldn't stop her skin from crawling at the thought of him touching her again. He had octopus hands. Clammy, searching and everywhere. *Everywhere!* His mouth acting like a Hoover vacuum on her lips and body making her feel like a dirty carpet. He told her she needed to "relax" more. Perhaps he was right. But dancing with him wouldn't help her do that.

"No," Erin said, hoping she didn't sound repulsed by the idea. "You dance with him."

"With pleasure." Caitlin handed Erin her champagne glass and sauntered towards Jeremiah, quickly getting his attention with her hip swishing walk and pretty smile. *Go Caitlin.* She'd keep him busy for awhile.

Erin set the glasses on an empty table and hugged herself. She felt restless and edgy. Lost without someone to talk to. She took a deep breath. She'd made it through the ceremony, with Jeremiah's hand sliding up and down her thigh, and now she only had to endure a couple hours for the reception. Normal. Act normal. Do not think about work. Do not imagine catastrophes. Empty your mind.

"Where did you dig this one up from?" a deep voice said from beside her.

Erin grinned at the disgust in her older brother's voice. He sounded as if she'd brought something from the ER disposal with her. She wanted to hug him. She wasn't the only one who saw that Jeremiah was completely self-absorbed. She wasn't crazy. She looked up at her brother and beamed. "So you wouldn't be disappointed if we broke up after tonight?"

"I'd be relieved."

She released a happy sigh.

"Mum would be in tears though."

Her sigh turned sad.

"Dad would worry."

She hung her head.

"Is that why you dressed in black?"

Her head snapped up. She shot him a look. "It's dark green." She held out her arms so that it could be seen clearly under the lights. "My dress is dark green."

He shrugged. "If you say so."

She let her arms fall to her sides. "Mum really likes him."

"But she'll get over it. They always do." He nodded towards Jeremiah. "You've got to stop doing this."

"Doing what?"

"Going out with guys like that."

She rested a hand on her chest. "It's not my fault. He asked me out."

"That's your problem. You need to go out with someone you like."

"He hasn't come around yet."

"Have you ever thought of asking him first?"

"He'll probably say no."

Brandon affectionately rubbed her head. "You're adorable."

Erin pushed his hand away. "Watch the hair."

He smiled. Her comment was a running joke between them. Her short afro was rarely ruffled.

"I think you deserve better than that," he said looking in Jeremiah's direction. "Instead of taking what comes to you, go after what you want. You did it with your career, do it with your life too."

"What brought this on?"

He sent her a long look. "I hate seeing you looking miserable."

"Do I look that bad? I thought I was hiding it well."

"I know you," he said in a serious tone. "This is what I want you to do. Over the next week I want you to ask a guy out."

"I'm too busy."

"You're not too busy. You're scared, but that's okay. Ask someone out and I'll take the blame for you breaking up with Jeremiah."

"You?"

He nodded.

"You'd do that for me?"

He nodded again.

She hugged him and kissed him on the cheek. "I love you."

He grinned. "I haven't done it yet. You have to do your part first."

She rolled her eyes. "Oh that's right."

"I believe in you."

"It won't be easy."

"I didn't say it would be." He sent Jeremiah a look. "Or you can stay with guys like him."

She groaned.

He patted her on the back. "One week." He looked around. "There are some single guys here so the clock starts now."

CHAPTER 4

He needed a good target.

Trent scanned the reception hall for possibilities as the light musical sound from a steel pan drifted through the air. He had to think like his brother. If he were to think like himself he'd only look at women who were alone or chatting with other women. But Xavier would see every woman as fair game. Ring-no ring (Trent wouldn't even pretend that he could go that far. He was not targeting a married or engaged woman). With kids—child free (Another no. He wouldn't want any kid to become attached to him no matter how brief. And he certainly wouldn't choose anyone expecting. Xavier specialized in women who were single and pregnant. "Try to get them in the second trimester when they just think they're fat. Call them beautiful and they'll be all over you," he liked to tell him.)

Trent inwardly groaned. No, he wasn't doing that either. He had his principles. He needed to prove his point with someone who would be easy, fast and provide a clean break. No obligations. No worries. No real heart-break. Just one month and then they would be finished.

Trent let his gaze survey the crowd as he considered the selection of ladies—Ring, Ring, Expecting, Too young, No ring but desperate. He paused. The woman in the purple dress was a possibility. She had a hungry I-want-to-be-married look that kept most guys away, but that could be an advantage he could use in his favor. But she'd be devastated when he broke up with her. No, he needed someone more resilient, but just as willing.

His gaze drifted further then landed on a woman standing alone hugging herself. She looked...bouncy. He didn't see a ring. She didn't look desperate. She looked...bored. Bouncy and bored. A strange, intriguing combina-tion. Cute with a short afro and arresting features. The right age, the right look. The perfect target.

"Forget about her," Mindy said with a shake of her head.

He turned to her surprised and annoyed that she could read him so well. "Forget about who?" he asked, trying to play it cool.

She nodded at the woman in the shift dress. "You're thinking of going after her, right?"

"Yes, so what?"

"I saw her come in with him." She gesture to a good looking man dancing with a laughing woman with hypnotic hips.

Trent hesitated and softly swore, surprised by how disappointed he felt. He was set on going after her. And now there was an obstacle. *I don't see one*, he could hear his brother say. *She's not dancing with him now and there's no ring. Go for it.* Trent lifted his chin. Tonight he was Xavier. If he could steal her away from a guy like that, it would be even better. "This is good."

Mindy sent him a curious glance. "What do you mean?"

"She's not even looking at the couple. She looks bored, which means she's not really invested in the relationship and may want some attention from someone else." He tugged on the cuffs of his jacket and took a step forward. "I'm going in."

"There's one more thing."

He paused. "What?"

"She's Derrick's cousin."

He shrugged and took another step forward. Great Dorothy would see he'd moved on. Even better. "Fine."

"And there's something else."

He clenched his teeth then spun around to her. "I thought you said there was only one more."

Mindy blinked, unapologetic. "You'll want to hear this."

Trent folded his arms, eager to put his plan into action. He sighed, feigning patience. "What is it?"

"She's a doctor."

His arms fell to his side. "You're kidding."

She shook her head. "Nope."

"Are you sure?"

"Positive. I heard someone mention it."

"What kind?"

"I didn't get that far."

He swore. He'd vowed never to date a doctor. He

came from a family of doctors. He made it a rule never to get involved with one. He slowly turned and stared at his possible target once more. He'd come up with that rule for a reason.

Then again, dating a doctor may be good since he would never fall for her. Ever. He'd see her for just a couple of weeks to prove his point, win a thousand dollars then get on with his life.

She'd prove an interesting challenge.

Mindy patted him on the back. "Never mind. You can find someone else. Or if you'll let me, I know of a great woman you might like to meet."

He opened his mouth to respond then he caught Dorothy's eye. She sent him a warm smile, but in her soft brown gaze he saw her pity. He didn't want her pity. Didn't need it. Or Mindy patting him like an affectionate pet that had lost its favorite toy.

He was a grown man. He wanted to be respected, admired. Desired. He looked at the cute doctor again and gritted his teeth. He was going to win this bet. He was going to get her number tonight and within a month she'd want them to be exclusive.

He saw Dorothy heading in his direction and knew he had to act. He knew what she'd say; he didn't want to hear it. The old Trent was gone. It was time to show her—show everyone—the kind of man he could be. He was getting out of the friend-zone tonight. For the next month he was going to make a woman want him. Bad.

"What are you doing?" Mindy called after him.

Trent flashed a smile over his shoulder before he winked. "I'm getting myself a doctor."

Mindy watched in awe as Trent crossed the room. The wink and smile he'd sent her was all cool, calculated sexiness and pure Xavier. She almost regretted making the bet and felt a little sorry for his target. The Brewster charm was difficult to resist and few had.

But that wasn't what truly worried her. She didn't want him to be right. She didn't want him to prove to her that women could be so easily manipulated. She knew some could, but others couldn't. He had to be patient. She was certain there was someone out there who would like him for himself. Trent knew how to channel his suave brother Xavier, she only hoped he didn't take it too far.

She folded her arms as she watched him make his way over to the doctor. He didn't look like himself and moved with a confidence she'd never seen before.

"What is he up to?"

Mindy jumped at the sound of Dorothy's voice. She hadn't heard her approach. "What do you mean?"

"He seems...different somehow."

Mindy shrugged. She didn't like Dorothy. Never had. She felt Dorothy was selfish and had dragged her cousin along longer than necessary. It didn't take a woman two years to realize she wasn't in love with someone. Especially someone desperately in love with her.

She stole a look at Dorothy and saw the surprise on the other woman's face and something else she'd never seen before: Interest. As if she were seeing a man for the first time. A sexy man. A devastatingly sexy man. She stifled a grin. *Yes, eat your heart out. This is what you lost.* Mindy opened her mouth to say something to the effect of, "Perhaps you're now seeing him in a new light," but then she noticed Dorothy wasn't the only woman staring at Trent. He'd managed to catch the sudden attention of several other women. Mindy felt her heart sink. Damn she didn't want Trent to be right. But so far he was.

Mindy looked at the doctor and secretly hoped she'd be different, that she wouldn't fall for the smooth, shallow Brewster charm. But the look on the woman's face made her heart sink even more. If Trent won this bet Mindy feared she'd lose a lot more than a thousand dollars.

Her cousin would also lose his trust in women permanently.

CHAPTER 5

"Would you like to dance?"

Erin had a refusal on her lips, but when she turned to the sound of the voice, the words died on her lips as she looked at a man with the kindest eyes she'd ever seen. His voice didn't seem to match his eyes. Nothing seemed to. He was handsome, not strikingly so like Derrick, but attractive with a solid jaw and fine nose. His face didn't match his eyes either. He had a cold, superior expression. Distant. But his eyes gave him away.

Those eyes—brown, enticing, caring—were so beautifully warm she felt her heart do a back flip. He had eyes she couldn't turn away from, eyes that kept her almost hypnotized. There had to be a mistake. Guys like him did not approach her. Nice guys. Good guys. She'd been used to dismissive glances, superior gazes, predatory eyes. But not him. Had her luck finally changed?

"What color is my dress?"

He blinked. "Um...green."

Her eyes widened. She pulled at the skirt of her dress. "You see it too? You're the first person who doesn't think it's black. Did you ask me to dance?"

He nodded, looking briefly uncertain. But she didn't care, he'd gotten the color of her dress right and he'd asked her to dance. She wouldn't lose this opportunity.

"Good, I wanted to make sure." She took his hand and led him onto the dance floor before pulling him into a dancer's embrace. It was when she snaked her arm around his waist that she realized she'd goofed. She softly swore. He'd asked *her* to danced. She should have let him take the lead, but she'd been afraid that he'd change his mind and she hadn't wanted to give him a chance too. But she also couldn't be overeager. *Don't frighten him away.* "Sorry," she said with a laugh she hoped sounded lighthearted. "Let's try this again. I shouldn't have grabbed you like that." She began to take a step back, but he stopped her.

"I don't mind."

Heat stole throughout her body. She was in trouble. She liked this. She liked that he didn't make her feel bad or aggressive or awkward. She took a deep breath. *Don't ruin this. Don't scare him away. Act normal.*

But it was hard to act normal being so close to a man who felt so good. His arms weren't clinging, but loosely held around her. Confident, not possessive. Not showy.

He smelled good too. Very good. Like a warm heady fragrance she'd never smelled before. It almost made her giddy. "What's the cologne you're wearing?"

She felt him stiffen and she briefly wondered if she'd said the wrong thing. "I'm not wearing cologne," he said.

"Really."

"Uh-huh."

"Oh. Well you smell divine." She inhaled his scent once more. "I'm sorry, I couldn't help myself." She inhaled one more time. "Now I'll stop before I mimic a clothes detergent commercial."

"Okay," he said, but she wasn't sure if he sounded amused or annoyed and she was too nervous to look at his face. She briefly closed her eyes. She'd keep her mouth shut, dance and then everything would be alright. She wouldn't be overbearing.

"What's your name?"

"Trent Brewster." He paused. "Do you usually dance with your eyes closed?"

Her eyes flew open. She didn't realized he'd pulled far enough away from her to see her face. She saw a brief light of amusement in his gaze before she lowered her own. "Sorry."

"Don't apologize. I was just curious."

She blinked quickly, wondering how she could recover the situation. "Did you say your name was Brent?"

"No Trent. Brewster."

"I'm Erin Freeman." She looked around the room searching for her brother, hoping he could see her dancing with someone other than Jeremiah. "Do you know the bride or the groom?"

"The bride."

"Friend or family?"

"Friend."

Erin waited but he didn't seem inclined to reveal anything further. Oookay...So he wasn't very talkative. That was fine. She could take the hint.

"I know the groom. We're cousins. Derrick and I aren't exactly close but he and my brother are and I heard he was interested in Dorothy for a long time. He said she was dating a doormat and that the poor sucker didn't know he never had a chance with her. Is something wrong?" she asked when she felt him stiffen again.

"No," he said in a tight voice.

She looked at the ground. "Did I step on your foot or something?"

"No."

She raised her gaze. "But enough about the groom, what do you know about the bride?"

"Let's talk about something else."

"Like what?"

"Or we don't have to talk at all."

Erin opened her mouth to agree then stopped when she noticed a violent scar that traveled down his neck from his jaw. "How did you get that?"

"What?"

She nodded towards it. "That scar on your neck."

He paused. "Bar fight."

"No, you didn't. The angle is all wrong." She narrowed her eyes and leaned closer. He wasn't that much taller than her. "Although I guess it's possible if the attacker grabbed your face like this." She took his chin in one hand and tilted his head. "And jabbed it with a knife." With the other hand she mimed the motion. She bit her lip, peered closer and traced her finger along the length of the scar. It was a very nasty scar and must have a painful history. "But it doesn't look like a knife wound or even the jagged edge of a bottle."

"If you give me my chin back, I'll tell you the truth."

Erin heard laughter in his voice and realized that she'd taken his face and nearly tilted it to his opposite shoulder. She immediately let go. "I am so sorry. Curiosity is a failing of mine. One of many." She folded her arms. Curiosity about his scar wasn't the only thing that intrigued her. For some reason she liked being close to him, in his space. It wasn't just his lovely scent, but a feeling of comfort. Another man might be angry with her, but he'd sounded amused and that made her relax. She was rarely this relaxed with a man outside the hospital or office. "So what happened?"

He pulled her back into a dancer's embrace. "I irritated the wrong guy. He met me out in the parking lot and left his mark. But I gave as good as I got."

She looked at him for a long moment. Not believing a word. He didn't lie well. "Sounds like an interesting story, but it just doesn't seem to match the wound. Do you have a tattoo?"

"What?"

She pointed. "I noticed a dark discoloration near the hollow of your neck. A strange place for a tattoo."

"It's not a tattoo."

"Birthmark?"

He nodded.

"What shape?"

"What shape?"

This time she nodded.

He hesitated a moment then said, "I'd have to unbutton my shirt."

"Only one button."

"You sure I should?"

"That's okay, I'm a doctor."

He didn't smile, but a glint of humor warmed his eyes. "Then I'm in good hands."

"The best."

He undid the button then opened his collar enough to show her.

She leaned close. "It looks like a kiss."

He glanced down. "No, it doesn't."

She laughed. "I know. I wanted to see if you'd check."

He lifted his gaze and his eyes met and held hers.

Something intense coursed through her and made her breathing shallow. *Get a hold of yourself!* She licked her lip and looked at his birthmark again. It gave her a chance to study his physique, the great breadth of his shoulders, the smooth column of brown skin, even from the brief contact with him she knew he was beautifully made. Her fingers itched to trace more than just the length of his scar or the shape of his birthmark, but she had to control herself. If she was lucky, maybe one day she'd get a chance to, but for now they were still strangers. She cleared her throat. *Act normal.*

"Actually, it could be any oval shape you want it to be," she said hoping to sound nonchalant. "What do you think it looks like?"

"You ask a lot of questions."

She quickly waved her hands. "You're right. I'm sorry. It's just...never mind. I'm sorry."

"Don't be."

"I work in the ER and my mind doesn't stop sometimes when it should. I also help my sister-in-law, who's a short story writer, with ideas for potential injuries for her characters and I started writing a little too and it's fun. So I'll imagine scenarios and... I know that sounds awful, but —" She halted when he gave her hand a light squeeze.

"Calm down," he said in a soft voice.

"What?"

"You talk as if I'm running away from you. I'm right here and I'm not going anywhere so you can slow down."

She took a deep breath. He was right. She was talking with the speed of an auctioneer at a cattle show.

"I guess I'm a little nervous."

"Why?"

"Because the music stopped and we're still dancing."

He hadn't noticed. Trent looked around the nearly empty dance floor where people now chatted with each other waiting for the next song, amazed. How could he not have noticed that?

"Enough about me," Erin said. "What do you do?"

He felt heat stealing into his cheeks. He almost didn't want to tell her considering he hadn't heard the music end. "I'm a sound engineer."

To his relief she didn't laugh. Instead she nodded and said, "What type?"

Trent paused for a moment not knowing what to say. It was rare that anyone would ask for specifics. If he told her the truth it would sound a lot less interesting and tonight he couldn't afford that. He had to keep her interest. He decided to go a neutral route. "I work for SonTil Sounds."

Her eyes widened and her mouth fell open, the same

way when he'd told her her dress was green. "No," she said, drawing out the word. He wasn't sure if her reaction was good or bad.

"You've heard of it?"

She clasped her hands together in reverence. "I love them. Our hospital has two of their prototype designs. One in the pediatrics unit and the other in hospice. The patients really benefit from all they do. People have no idea how powerful sound can be when it comes to healing. People focus on medicine and the colors of the room. But our aural reflexes can't be ignored and SonTil Sounds is one of those innovative companies making great strides in audio technological advances. But of course you know that. What do you do there?"

For the second time in as many minutes Trent didn't know what to say. No one had ever shown this much interest in what he did. Most didn't even know about the company he'd co-founded with a friend. They were still a small company compared to most and what were the odds that he'd meet someone who worked at one of the hospitals that was using their creation?

Most women who heard he was a sound engineer thought he worked as a studio or recording engineer collaborating with artists and producers. They didn't realize he was a scientist. He worked in research and development and had studied psychoacoustics, or how humans respond to what they hear, and architectural acoustics, focusing on achieving quality sound within a room.

He'd briefly worked at a headphone manufacturer,

done another stint as a consultant before he started his own business and won a grant to do research and development that allowed him to create the OntheSpot wearable.

He never would have imagined he'd find his way back to medicine, even on a peripheral level, considering how much he hated being surrounded by doctors. He'd focused on everything but that realm—schools, universities, studios, stages, theaters—then he'd had a crisis.

Something he still couldn't mention even to himself, but he'd been in the hospital for the first time in years. A place he'd stayed away from.

Hospitals had been his life, tagging after one relative or another, down those hallowed halls, and when he'd been forced to return he remembered why he despised them. It was because he didn't like the sounds in them. The beeping monitors (that never seemed to stop), the squeak of soles on tile floors, the rolling cots and whir of automatic doors, but what was worse was the moaning or the consistent drone of voices of family members anxiously gathered in a waiting room or the intermittent sobs coming from patients' rooms.

And at night it could be worse. There was no quiet for people to rest and that could affect the healing process. Less than four years go he'd made it his mission to do something. He wanted to work on building a more harmonious environment. He knew that the present sounds in hospitals included too many alarms, not only jarring the environment's soundscape, but leading to nurses and other healthcare professionals becoming numb due to "alarm fatigue", which could lead to them failing to respond to alarms that were truly urgent and, in some cases, resulting in death.

So he designed a wearable that sent a silent alert to nurses when a patient's vitals changed. A silent alert instead of a loud alarm or beeping monitor and called it OnTheSpot.

His renewed interest in the hospital environment came at a time when a growing number of hospitals started to see patients as consumers plus design innovation began to focus on the end user (i.e. patient) experience, which helped to create a viable driving force to implement some of his ideas on a smaller scale and at small hospitals like Treeline.

He liked how her eyes lit up when she asked about his work. He'd never seen that kind of passion before. Ambition yes. Drive definitely. But not passion. And joy. She glowed.

He almost told her of another project they were working on called Last Sounds—asking people what sounds they'd like to hear before they die—like crashing waves, birds singing, shifting sand, a favorite song, or a family member's voice. Instead of ignoring someone's imminent death the goal was to highlight the possible beauty of one's end-of-life experience. But he kept his mouth closed. "You can go on too long sometimes" Dorothy liked to playfully chide him.

Erin laughed. A nervous laugh he was getting used to and smiled as if she'd done something wrong. "Is it top secret or something?"

It was then he realized he hadn't answered her question, having been so surprised by the beauty of her happy face. *Keep them guessing,* he could hear his father say. *Be a mystery,* his brother would add. "Something like that."

"Well, it's a pleasure to meet you all the same." She pulled him to the side. "I've got to show you something." She took out her cell phone and showed a smiling heavyset woman wearing the OnTheSpot device. "I don't get to see a lot of this in the ER, but a friend let me see it. I like to read up on as many things as I can and this innovation has just caught my imagination. This is only the beginning."

Trent swallowed, feeling his heart race. She kept talking about his work. That was one of his weaknesses. It could get him into trouble.

She's a doctor. Remember she's a doctor. They can be obsessive too. That's all. It's nothing personal. She could be talking to anyone. Trent bit his lip resisting the urge to expand on what he knew. He wanted to tell her how they'd come up with the idea, how long the design had taken, the years of failures. *No woman wants to hear that,* his father would tell him. *That's how you end up as friends,* his brother would add. He took a deep breath and softly swore. No, he wouldn't weaken. He knew what was in store. She was only responding to him like this because he was pretending to be someone else. If she knew the real Trent, she'd get bored and he'd be dancing at her wedding a year from now.

He'd prove his theory correct then leave and forget about her. Forget about everything. *Pretend you don't care. Draws them like moths,* his father liked to tell him.

He needed to focus on his mission and proceed to stage two. Get her number.

He began to pull out his cell phone. "Would you like to—"

"You two look cozy," Dorothy said behind them. "What are you staring at?"

CHAPTER 7

"Nothing," Trent said quickly, pushing Erin's phone out of view.

"A SonTil Sound invention," Erin said. "See?" She held up the screen then shook her head. "Not that there's anything to see here because the device is so small, but the smile says it all. OnTheSpot is simple but amazing. I hope other hospitals will get to benefit from what SonTil's doing."

Dorothy smiled. "Don't you think you're laying it on a bit thick?"

Erin frowned. "I don't understand."

"You don't need to butter him up. Trent's one of the easiest men to—"

Trent opened his mouth to interrupt her, but Erin spoke before he could.

"We don't know each other very well so I'm sure you're not trying to be offensive. Especially now that we're family." Erin put her cell phone away. "But to clarify, I am not trying to butter, spread or whatever kind of food reference you were trying to make. I was having what I thought was an interesting conversation with a man who works at one of my favorite places."

Dorothy's brows shot up in surprise. "Works there?" She looked at Trent. "He ow—"

"Owes them a lot of gratitude," Trent smoothly cut in. He pulled out his phone. "I don't want to take up any more of your time. Here's my phone number so we can chat later."

"Thanks," she said saving the number to her phone. Seconds later he heard the sound of thunder and rain which he'd set as the ringtone for his phone. Erin smiled then said, "And now you have mine," before she waved goodbye and left.

Dorothy frowned at him. "Why didn't you want her to know that you own the company?"

"If she's interested she can look me up and find out for herself." *Let them do the chasing. Don't give them everything up front.*

"But you love talking about your company and you can go on about..." She paused. "What was that again?" She tapped her chin. "It's on the tip of my tongue. "What did you study psycho-something or other?"

"Psychoacoustics."

She nodded pleased. "Yes, that's right. You'd talk about that for hours if I let you," she said with a laugh. "Remember when you—"

Trent shoved his hands in his pockets. "What do you want?"

Dorothy's gaze grew concerned. "What's going on with you? You're acting strange."

Dammit don't look at me like that. Like you care more than you really do. I fell for that look once. "What did you want to talk to me about?"

She blinked, surprised by his curt tone. "Do I need a reason to talk to my best friend?"

"When he's trying to get lucky? Yes."

Dorothy glanced at Erin who stood against a far wall and was studying one of the large chandeliers then looking at the people standing below it. "You're interested in her?" she asked unimpressed.

"That surprises you?"

"Yes. I mean look at her. What is she doing?"

Trent sent Erin a look then shrugged. "Probably imagining what she would do if the chandelier came loose and fell on those people."

Dorothy's mouth fell open. She turned to him shocked. "That's awful!"

He couldn't stop a grin. "I know."

"You think that's funny?"

He squeezed her tense shoulder. "Relax, it's not going to happen. Everything will be perfect."

She folded her arms. "You're just playing with me."

"No, I wanted her number and I got it."

"Did you know she's a doctor?"

"I plan to overlook it." *For now.*

She narrowed her eyes. "You're up to something. Don't ruin this for me."

"I'm not going to ruin anything."

She frowned. "I want to believe you, but I'm not sure.

You hate doctors. Dating one doesn't sound like you."

No, it wasn't like him at all, but that was what a challenge was for. In spite of himself he felt his gaze wander back to Erin and, amused, he studied her watching one of the steel pan musicians with a speculative look. Was she imagining one of them losing grip of their sticks and it flying across the room and hitting someone?

Dorothy suddenly jumped in front of him. "Trent."

He sighed strangely annoyed that she'd blocked his view. He looked at her. "What?"

"She's not your type."

"I've told you. I've changed." Before he could let his gaze drift away again, Dorothy lightly touched his hand, her fingers soft and warm. She lowered her voice to a low purr that always got his attention.

"I'm really glad you could come."

He blinked irritated that she still knew how to get to him. "So you've said."

She wrapped her fingers around his hand and the sweet scent of violets wafted towards him again. "I wasn't sure you would considering how much we mean to each other." She held his gaze. "I know how hard this is for you."

It was the word "hard" that pulled him from under her spell and sent him spinning back to the past when he lay naked in his bed hearing her tell him she didn't love him. He remembered how briefly, stupidly, he'd thought that if they were friends, maybe he could win her back.

And he felt the pain of the day—the silence as Derrick slipped a ring on her finger, the sound of applause as they left the church as husband and wife—

crash over him like a tidal wave. He felt himself drowning in the swirling, depthless feeling of loss.

"Don't do anything rash," she continued, her soft brown eyes searching his. "One day I want to see you as happy as I am."

Trent jumped when he felt a hard grip wrap around his forearm and yank him back. "He's happy," Mindy said.

Dorothy sniffed. "Maybe."

"Excuse us." She dragged him away.

"What are you doing?" Trent asked as he let her lead him to an empty table.

"Getting you away from her." She pushed him into a chair.

"You don't need to do that."

"Of course I do." She sat down beside him and kicked him under the table. "You had that look again."

"No, I didn't."

Mindy waved her finger. "But that's not all. She made a beeline to you and that doctor."

"I know, which is weird."

"She looked jealous."

Trent shook his head and laughed amused. "She wasn't jealous. Dorothy just doesn't like to be left out of things. She was curious about what we were looking at."

Mindy's voice remained firm. "She was jealous. I was watching that doctor talk to you."

"Her name is Erin."

"What?"

"She's not 'that doctor'. Her name is Erin."

"It doesn't matter what her name is. She got you to

unbutton your shirt."

Trent felt his face grow hot as he remembered the touch of Erin's finger on his skin. He redid the button. "She was interested in my scar."

"Plus you should have seen your face. At one point you looked like someone had given you the Presidential Medal of Freedom or something."

Trent ran a hand down his face and swore. He'd thought he'd covered his emotions better than that. "Think she noticed?"

"Of course she noticed that's why she came over to you."

He shook his head. "Not Dorothy. Erin."

Mindy thought for a moment then shrugged. "Doubt it. She was too busy looking at what was on her phone. What were you two looking at anyway?"

"She's a fan of my work. She showed me one of the nurses at her hospital using the OnTheSpot device."

"And you told her you designed it?"

"No, it's something she'll discover on her own."

Mindy folded her arms. "I don't think you're playing fair. You shouldn't lie about your business."

"Omission isn't the same as a lie."

"Close."

He lifted a sly brow. "I'm being Xavier, remember?"

She shivered. "You do that too well. I've changed my mind. Forget the bet. I think—"

He held up his hand. "Too late. I've already gone this far. I plan to finish this and win."

Mindy sat back defeated. "Erin may be different," she said with a tinge of hope.

"She's not."

Mindy fell silent a moment then said, "What's your next move?"

"I've made it. It's her turn now."

"What do you mean?"

Trent leaned forward and lowered his voice. "This is what's going to happen. She's going to seek me out, do an online search, be impressed by what she finds which will increase her interest in me. Then she'll contact me. After that I'll take it from there. However, if I lay it all out now then there's no mystery left and I end up where I've always been."

"A real woman doesn't need mystery. You're an amazing guy. I think—"

"I don't date doctors," he said in a flat tone. "Ever."

Mindy rolled her eyes. "That's a stupid rule."

"Stupid? You try growing up with a pediatric surgeon, a thoracic surgeon, a urologist and gynecologist. I know how doctors think. I wouldn't date one for real and I definitely, absolutely wouldn't marry one. I want a life separate from medicine."

Mindy's voice grew impatient. "Trent—"

He smiled without humor. "You know, she actually asked about my scar and when I told her I got it in a bar fight she was curious about what kind of knife was used or if it was a broken bottle."

Mindy frowned. "Okay, that is strange."

"No, it's typical. Doctors aren't like the rest of us."

"But you shouldn't have lied to her." She held up her hand. "This time it wasn't omission it was a flat out lie. Why didn't you tell her how you really got your scar?"

He rested his chin in his hand. "A bar fight makes a better story than a school bus crash." He'd been in his junior year of high school on a trip with his band when their bus collided with a semi truck. The truck driver had suffered a coronary and lost consciousness, sliding into oncoming traffic.

Fortunately, no lives were lost, but he'd ended up critically wounded and had been rushed to the hospital with six others. He was the only student who had no parental visitors. He'd later learned that his father had called to find out his condition and once he and his mother knew Trent wasn't going to die they continued with their schedule. His father had an early morning surgery and his mother had a speaking engagement. His older brother had an exam he couldn't—or wouldn't reschedule—while his sister was abroad so he didn't expect anything from her.

It was his aunt—Mindy's mother—who'd come to see him and looked after him until he was released.

It wasn't that his family was cruel, but apathetic. He'd learned that doctors didn't go into the profession because they cared. His Jamaican-born father liked how saving lives stroked his ego, his British-born, Canadian raised mother liked the money and prestige; his brother enjoyed the competitive nature of the field and his sister followed in the predetermined footsteps set out for her. At a young age it was clear that Trent was different than the rest. His aunt liked to remind him of the time when he was five years old and she'd taken him and Mindy to story time at the local library.

When the librarian was reading a picture book about

different professions and said, "Doctors are nice and heal you" he'd burst out laughing. He'd laughed so long and loud that his aunt had to take him out of the room.

"But it's not true," he said hurt that he'd been scolded for disrupting the reading. He pointed to the band aid on his knee. "I put this on myself."

He was always patching up his own scrapped knees. His mother told him to clean the wound and kept the First Aid Kit on the bottom shelf for him to reach. "Take care of yourself so that we can look after others," was her motto.

Family gatherings were always a strain. Everyone was "Dr. Brewster" (even his two stepmothers—one a GP; the other a podiatrist) except for him and myopically focused on all things medical. He could tell by the brief chat with Erin that she would easily fall into the same line as his family and he set out to keep as much distance between him and them as he could.

"You can't win this by lying to her." When Trent sent her a knowing look, she relented and said, "Xavier doesn't always lie."

"Most times. Besides, she doesn't need to know too much about me." He remembered sharing the trauma of the bus crash with his college girlfriend to explain why he'd wanted to travel to New York by train. She'd giggled and said he was being silly and that bus crashes were rare. He didn't feel like exposing himself to that kind of ridicule again. "And I'll make sure she doesn't find out much at all."

CHAPTER 8

He didn't expect to still be thinking about her.

Trent sat in the control room of Tran Street Studio with his friend Vince as they both listened to a mixed track for the song "Putcha Hands On Me" by local rap artist, Yula, who sat beside him, bobbing his head from side to side. But he couldn't focus on the song or anything else. In his mind he heard the sound of Erin's laughter. It was nervous and shy and genuine. And he wondered how true it would be if she hadn't been so awkward with him. But she hadn't been awkward enough not to touch him and he wondered why he let her.

Because you liked it, a little voice said and he admitted that he did. Although it didn't make sense. He didn't like anyone to focus on his scar, but for some reason Erin had been different. Perhaps it was her analytical interest, he could understand that. He had strange curiosities too. He wondered how long it would take for her to look him up. He expected her to call him by that afternoon. Then again, he didn't know her schedule so he might have to wait another day.

He didn't want to wait long.

A loud clap wretched him from his thoughts and he realized the song had ended.

Yula jumped up from his chair. He was as skinny as a string bean and looked about twelve, but he had a powerful mastery with words and a voice to follow. He was a twenty-year-old economics major who had been pursuing his music for the past six years and was slowly making waves online and around the city. "Hey K-Pop, how come I sound like I'm talking under water?" Yula asked.

Vince swore and said politely, "Because you sound like a puffer fish on crack."

Yula laughed. "Nah."

"It's the effect when you swallow your words like that, but I can work on it."

He patted him on the back and said, "Thanks K-Pop. See ya!" before he sauntered out of the control room.

Vince stared through the window at the now empty studio where a series of microphones sat. He sighed. "I hate that guy."

Trent sat back in his seat glancing at the digital audio workstation to his right. "Why, K-Pop?" he said using Yula's nickname for him.

Vince flashed him a rude gesture.

Although of Vietnamese, not Korean, background with his sharp, stylish clothes and dyed brown haircut (that he frequently changed), Vince could be the older double of a top performer singer, songwriter and actor V. Yula mentioned his sister had fallen for the singer who was part of the popular South Korean boy band BTS. But what truly annoyed Vince about the nickname was that he didn't do pop music of any kind but had performed in the rap world for a decade before ending up on the engineering and production end.

Trent had met Vince in Bali when Vince was an up and coming rap artist and Trent was interning with a small acoustics company helping with the sound system for a concert. They immediately hit it off and kept in touch. Vince found it difficult to make waves stateside, although he'd been born in Florida, but ended up having a lucrative career abroad.

When Vince returned to the States, Trent had encouraged him to think about expanding his interest in audio engineering since he'd asked a lot of questions about production during each concert and sound recording. Vince had at first hesitated, since he hadn't done well in math in school, but with persistence and loads of study he eventually opened up Tran Street Studio a very profitable recording studio that offered mixing and mastering as an option, whether someone used his studio to record or not. He promised the highest quality sound and offered studio sessions with or without an engineer.

Although Trent didn't work there, if he had the time and Vince asked him to stop by and listen in, he was always willing to do so. Especially when characters like Yula showed up.

"If you don't like him, stop working with him."

"I don't hate him enough to not want to take his money."

"You make enough."

Vince shrugged. "I guess I don't hate the kid as much as I should. Thanks for stopping by."

"You didn't really need my input."

He rubbed his hands together. "I need a favor."

"I'm busy."

Vince grinned at Trent's quick reply.

Aside from recording, Tran Street Studio also offered classes in the tools and techniques one can apply to home recording projects. In the beginning, Trent had taught two one-on-one sessions with women who wanted to take their lessons a lot further than he wanted to. He'd stayed away since.

"No, it's not that," Vince said. "It's Sally. Her antique store is in trouble. I know you don't do consulting any more but—"

Trent relaxed and nodded. "I'll see what I can do."

"Thanks, man." He stood and hit him on the back. "Let's get something to drink."

Minutes later they settled in a bustling café, catering to professionals and college students who'd never had to work a day in their lives, located two blocks away from the studio. They sat at a table surrounded by the scent of banana nut bagels and two cups of coffee in front of them. Vince had few vices anymore since giving up his party boy ways, except for black coffee, which he could consume by the gallons. The dragon tattoo on Vince's forearm seemed to undulate as he lifted his cup. "So how was the funeral?"

Trent frowned. "I didn't attend a funeral."

"I thought you were going to Dorothy's wedding this weekend."

Trent made the connection. Her wedding, his funeral. "Very funny."

Vince lifted a brow. "Her wedding was funny?"

"Sure, K-Pop it was hilarious."

Vince took a long sip of his drink then slowly set it down. "Call me that one more time and I will hurt you."

Trent met his gaze unfazed and smiled. "Don't think I'm not itching for a fight."

Vince lowered his gaze and shook his head, understanding the warning. Trent wasn't happy and would kindly take to punching someone's face in if provoked. "I think you're a brave man. If an ex of mine asked me to come to her wedding she better be ready to see her cake set on fire with a blowtorch."

Trent folded his arms. "It wasn't that bad."

Vince stroked the side of his cheek. "And yet you still wanted to rearrange my handsome face."

"The feeling comes and goes." He sighed. "I'm happy for her."

Vince choked on his coffee. "Are you trying to make me sick? Stop lying."

"I'm not lying." Much. "The wedding was great and at the reception there were—"

Vince closed his eyes. "Unless you're about to tell me there were a series of topless dancers I'm not interested." He opened his eyes. "She's your *ex*, man. Your ex. And she invited you to her wedding and you went! You got a new suit, you bought a present, and you went. I still can't believe it."

"We're friends."

"No, she's—" He stopped and bit his lip. "Cut her out now."

"Exes can be friends."

"Sure, but not you. You still love her. Everyone knows how much—except her."

"I'm getting over her."

Vince sent him a long, considering look. "Let me help you speed up the process. I've got a friend." He sat back with a smug grin. "One night with her and—"

"I'm not interested."

"At least let me finish."

"No."

Vince shook his head. "Sometimes I don't know how we remain friends."

"You take her out for me."

Vince shot him a look. "You know I'm a married man."

"Happily married," Trent said, referring to Vince's wife, Lana Lee, a third generation Marylander and makeup artist he'd met while touring.

"I'm married. Being happy has nothing to do with it."

"But you are."

Vince looked around as if he feared being overheard, but couldn't stop a smile from reaching his lips. "Keep that to yourself."

"I'll keep your friend in mind, but...I'll be busy for the next month."

Vince looked at him then swore. "You met somebody

at the funeral?" When Trent shot him a look he shrugged. "I don't care, I'm not calling it a wedding. So what she like? When are you seeing her again?"

"Don't know."

He frowned. "You don't know?"

"I'm taking things slow this time. I'm testing a theory."

"You're dealing with women. That could be dangerous."

"It won't be. I know what I'm doing."

"That's not the danger. It's what will happen when she finds out what you're doing."

"She won't."

"I hope you're right."

"I know I am."

But he wasn't sure when a couple days passed and Erin hadn't contacted him. His brother would have gotten a call by now. Hadn't she looked him up yet? Seen that he was the owner of SonTil Sounds? Had her interest been a lie? Just hollow flattery?

That Monday evening he drove home from work searching his mind. Where could he have gone wrong? He'd read her right, he'd been certain of it. Was she waiting for him to call? But then that meant he was chasing her and not the other way around. He had to be disinterested and nonchalant. But Mindy sounded triumphant on the phone when he reluctantly admitted that she hadn't contacted him yet.

"See? Not everyone falls for the Xavier act."

Erin's pretty face rose in his mind. He'd chosen well. He hadn't made a mistake. "She will."

CHAPTER 9

But she hadn't and he started to worry.

Really worry.

It had been nearly a week.

Trent walked into his kitchen late that Thursday to fix a snack. He had started to pour ginger beer into a glass when he heard a soft whimper, then a whine. He turned and saw his brown Lab, Roger, with his red leash in his mouth and a particular look in his eyes. Trent knew that look. That look meant trouble. He shook his head. "No, not today. It's too early and I've got too much on my mind." He glanced at the time. "Wait twenty minutes and we'll go on our regular walk." He paused. "Don't look at me like that."

Roger whimpered and blinked.

Trent turned away. He knew if he let Roger persuade him then the rest of the day would be ruined. He wasn't in the mood. He was still getting over the wedding (Dorothy as a beautiful happy bride), and the silence

(Why hadn't Erin contacted him yet?) He just wanted to stay home and do nothing but watch a couple shows.

Roger whined again.

"I haven't even eaten anything yet."

Roger put the leash next to Trent's foot.

Trent sighed and picked it up. Roger's tail began to wag in anticipation; he even looked like he was smiling.

"Just this once."

Trent always said that but it wasn't true. "Fine, let me get my gear."

He let Roger lead the way since he knew his dog was on a mission. He'd moved from an apartment in the city, which had a thriving dog park, to a small house in the suburbs, hoping that there would be less to distract Roger who could become over stimulated. Most people thought he'd moved because he didn't want to remember all the time he'd spent with Dorothy at his apartment since the move came soon after their breakup. They were only partly right about his motivations, but Trent had also been ready to settle down and bought the brick, split-level house he'd hoped to share with her. He was moving on with his life in his own way even if it was with his six-year-old dog.

The move had seemed to work for a couple of weeks, but not as much as he'd hoped. Roger had returned to his old habit.

Roger hurried his way down the paved sidewalk shaded under trees and carefully mowed lawns until they reached the main street. The roar of a bus barreling past didn't distract Roger as he continued to charge ahead. They walked about three more blocks when Roger stopped and looked up at him. Trent sighed and released his leash. "Okay, go on."

Trent sat on the curb and watched Roger disappear between two houses. Moments later he came back with a little black kitten in his mouth.

The kitten was in terrible shape. Roger put it on the towel Trent had brought with him and placed on the ground. The kitten made a soft sound but barely raised its head. Trent gave Roger a pat on the head. "Good job." He wrapped the kitten up. "If we hadn't come this little guy would have been a hawk's dinner."

"What a cute little girl," Mindy told Trent the following day when he returned to the shelter to check on the kitten's progress. His cousin was the administrator of the SandHill Animal Shelter and was used to Roger's various finds. The kitten had gone through the rounds with the vet and was deemed to be underweight but without any disease so it would be put on the adoption floor. They presently stood in the area outside the clinic surrounded by animal cages. The sound of barking, soft cries and snoring (from a tired boxer) filled the air. Trent held and stroked the kitten on the head and it began to purr.

Mindy grinned. "Kittens usually go fast, but...if you could keep her it would be great. She likes you."

Trent continued to stroke the soft fur, feeling the delighted purring vibrating against his chest. "Why would you want me to keep her?"

"Black cats don't get adopted as fast."

Trent softly swore. Damn superstitions. He held up the kitten. It blinked its grey eyes. He turned the kitten to face Mindy. "Who could resist this face?"

Mindy looked at Trent, a speculative expression crossing her face. "Hold that pose. I'm going to take a picture. I think you'll help too."

"Me?"

"Yes. I said don't move. Yes, hold her close to your face like that. Perfect." She held up her cell phone and took a picture then looked down at the image. "Perfect."

Trent looked at the image over her shoulder. "Yes, what a cutie."

"So's the cat."

Trent nudged her with his elbow. "Shut up."

"I'm serious. With you in the picture it will help her."

"How is a black guy supposed to help a black cat? Please don't tell me you'll talk about going beyond skin deep."

She hit him on the back of the head. "You're so clueless."

"Ow. What did I say?"

She pointed to the screen. "This image shows a sweet, good looking guy who found this adorable kitten who needs a good home. With a story like that this girl will find someone eager to take her home."

Trent nodded. "Oh, that makes sense."

"You shouldn't sell yourself short. So has the doctor called you yet?"

He cleared his throat and placed the kitten back in the cage. "Not yet."

"What will you do if she doesn't?"

"She will."

Mindy grinned. "If she doesn't, I win."

"You won't win. If she doesn't call, I have another tactic that will work," Trent said with more conviction than he felt.

CHAPTER 10

"You don't really need me to help you do this," Erin said as she scrolled through the animal shelter photos posted online. She'd just come off her shift at the hospital and had stopped by the apartment her brother and sister-in-law shared. It wasn't a far commute since they were only one building away from hers. They sat in the living room with signs of the couple's professions as a writer and data processor, respectively, everywhere—Tara's latest short story collection sat on the coffee table and pages of what looked like gibberish lay on a side chair as Erin went through the images, her brother and sister-in-law sitting on either side of her.

Brandon stared at a movie on the flat screen, pretending he didn't care, while Tara sighed at every image, resting her chin on Erin's shoulder. "If I could, I'd adopt them all," she said.

"That's why I called Erin," Brandon said, chewing on a plantain chip.

Erin shook her head. "I still don't think you need me."

"We do," Tara said. "You have a way of seeing things we miss. You helped us find Vienna."

It wasn't purely an accident. For some reason she had an ability to match animals and people. Growing up she'd been in charge of selecting the family pet and her selections always suited them. Erin saw it as a useless ability but her brother liked it. She'd paired her aunt with a cockatoo she'd had for the past eight years; their parents owned a calm mixed breed dog named Toro she had selected for them that they'd had for fifteen years.

Brandon and Tara had lost their twelve-year-old calico, Vienna, last year and were ready to offer another cat a new home.

"You can't tell everything from only a photo anyway," Erin said. "I'd prefer to visit in-person."

"You don't have the time and I'll go later. And...oh no...Stop! I'm in love."

"Again," Brandon said in a bored voice.

"I mean it this time." Tara pointed at the screen. "He's adorable."

Erin looked at the image and gasped.

"I know. What a story. Oh...it's a 'she'. She was found near death and it says she's incredible sweet."

Erin blinked quickly, unable to believe her eyes. "I know that man."

"Really?"

"Sort of. I met him at Dorothy's wedding. Brandon look."

Brandon glanced at the image with little interest. "What?"

"Remember him?"

"No."

"I saw him at Derrick's wedding."

"There were a lot of people there," he said still sounding bored. "I don't remember him."

Erin frowned. "I don't blame you. He looks so different here." But his eyes were the same. She'd never forget those beautiful, kind brown eyes.

"Different how?" Tara asked.

Erin shook her head. "I don't know. Friendlier somehow. We have to get this kitten."

Brandon sent her a knowing look. "The man isn't included."

She playfully punched him in the arm. "I know that."

He stood with a smile. "Just making sure. And the week's almost up."

Her heart picked up pace. She'd been stalling. She'd hoped he would have called her, but every day ended with disappointment. Would she really have to take the lead? "I know that too."

MINDY SUSPECTED USING TRENT'S PHOTO WOULD help the little kitten's chances but she had no idea the deluge of offers she'd receive from both near and far. Now she had to make sure that the kitten went to the right home.

This week she'd had returns (rare but always devastating) of two dogs—a German Sheppard mix and a boxer —and didn't want the same to happen to the kitten who they'd named Sunny. She would have to trust her instincts.

The moment a man and woman walked through the main entrance hall she knew that if they wanted the black kitten, she'd have to say no. She didn't usually deal with the public, but the kitten was special and had already shown a personality of being very quiet and needing calm. But the tall woman with the short afro dressed in a fitted orange T-shirt and black trousers had a bottled energy as if she were a rocket ready to set off. However the man beside her had a calmer, steady presence so it could work. For some reason the woman looked familiar. Where had she seen her before?

"We'd like to see Sunny," the woman said. Even her voice set Mindy a little on edge. It was sharp, direct, uncompromising. "Which is a great irony by the way," she continued. "Sunny for a black cat. You'd expect it to be called Midnight or something. Who came up with that? You? The guy who found her or another staff member here?"

"I did," Mindy said unsettled. She was the one used to asking questions not the other way round.

"Does she have any particular habits? Or temperament? I know you said she was sweet but that could mean anything." She looked around at the clear main foyer and smiled at a mural of a series of different cats and dogs. "I used to volunteer at a shelter and I must say this is one of the best I've seen. You must be very proud, but I was just curious about—"

The man beside her rested an arm around the woman's shoulders and flashed a smile as white and sweet as a marshmallow. "As you can see we were impressed with the story."

Mindy felt herself relax. If this man was the woman's husband he knew how to offset her intense energy. Where had she seen her before? Who did she remind her of? "You and lots of others. Don't get your hopes up. I think we already have an adoption underway."

"Just one look, please."

Mindy relented and took them to the back. The kitten was shy and would likely stay in the corner, staring out at them with wide grey eyes, as it had for other visitors.

And as expected she did just that until something remarkable happened. The woman pursed her lips and made a slight clicking sound then said, "Come on," and the kitten's ears twitched then it slowly crept forward until it pressed its head against her finger.

Mindy had never witnessed anything like it. She'd seen others cooing at the cat, talking in soft tones, high pitched tones, baby tones and the kitten hadn't moved but this odd woman had gotten the kitten to come to her and...was it purring? She felt awful for making such a snap judgment. Clearly the woman wasn't as off-putting as she first appeared. Which made her think of Trent. People saw his easygoing, quiet endearing way as a weakness and missed how amazing he was. Trent. Why did this woman make her think of him?

Was it because Sunny purred loudly when she held her? No, that wasn't it. There was something else. A deeper tie. She looked so... Yes, the wedding! This was the woman he'd been speaking to. Erin something.

Mindy shifted her gaze to the man by her side. He also seemed familiar. Had he been at the wedding too? Was she seeing someone else already? Was that why she hadn't called? Had Trent already lost? She felt a little angry on his behalf. Couldn't she have given him a chance? Then again the Trent Erin had met at Dorothy's wedding wasn't the one Mindy knew and loved. Trent had pulled an Xavier act and been cagey and misleading. Perhaps that had been a turn off. She couldn't blame her for moving on.

Mindy sighed. She didn't mind winning the bet if it meant that Trent would go back to being himself and take the time to find the woman who was really right for him.

"We'll take him right now," the man said. "If there's a chance."

"I have to talk to a few people first. Wait here." But she knew it was a done deal. Her instincts told her that Sunny had found a new home and that would be Trent's consolation prize for losing.

CHAPTER 11

"How many times have I told you not to do that?" Brandon softly chided as he crossed the hot parking lot carrying the kitten in its new carrier.

Erin looked at him surprised that she was in trouble. "What?"

"I've told you not to talk like an interrogator." He opened the back door of his black Nissan and settled the carrier inside the backseat.

"I didn't."

"You should have seen that poor woman's face."

"I did look at it. I complimented her and—"

He closed the door. "She looked shell-shocked." He sat in the driver's seat and immediately turned on the air conditioner. "I know you mean well, but you can't treat people like patients who've come through the emergency room. What happened? What are the vitals? Which bed is free?"

Erin grabbed the seatbelt then snatched her hand back when she touched the hot metal. She shook her hand then pulled the strap and grumbled, "I don't sound like that."

"Close." He squeezed her shoulder. "Try to relax a little. You can be a bit...overwhelming."

"I don't mean to be. I was...never mind."

Brandon looked behind him and began to back out of the parking space. "The right guy won't be scared off."

"He didn't call."

"I told you to call him."

"What's the point? I can't change. I don't want to."

Brandon drove the car into another empty space then turned to her. "I didn't ask you to change yourself. Just your pattern."

"Jeremiah wants to—"

Brandon covered her mouth. "Break up with him."

She removed his hand. "But—"

"I mean it."

"We're not really a couple."

"I don't care what you are. Stop seeing him."

"At least I don't scare him."

"True, but he scares me."

Erin giggled. "I know. Isn't he awful? He once left a waiter in tears." She looked back at Sunny asleep in her carrier. "If only men were like animals."

"Some men are."

She turned to him. "Dogs?"

He flashed a sour grin. "Maybe you deserve to be with Jeremiah."

She pinched his cheek. "Just kidding. At least animals like me. Animals understand me."

"I don't know how you do it but try to approach people the same way."

"She's a sweetie. Only sweet animals trust me."

"At first I wasn't sure that woman would even let us see the cat."

"I know." Erin looked at Sunny. "So I had to win her over." It was her best defense; she'd been told she could be a little intimidating. She'd learned that by being good with animals that they could help her cut through the ice with people. She'd made a lot of summer money by watching other people's pets. They'd learned to trust her and what people, at times, thought of as strange ways worked for her with animals. But she'd gotten Brandon and Tara a new family member and learned that the guy at the wedding was as kind as she'd suspected him to be. He hadn't called. No surprise there. But, she had his number...

CHAPTER 12

"You lost."

Trent stared at Mindy who stood on his doorstep holding up a bottle of wine. She had a sad expression on her face.

"What?"

She stepped past him, gave Roger a quick pat on the head then hung up her coat on the coat rack. "The good news is that I already know who I want you to meet first."

Trent closed the door. "What do you mean 'I lost'?"

She went to his kitchen and took down some wine glasses. She set them on the counter. "You would not believe who adopted Sunny."

"Probably not. But what does that have to do with me losing?"

"I'm getting to that." She opened the bottle. "Be patient."

She poured the red wine into the glasses then left the kitchen and sat at the dining table. "Now guess."

Trent sat down in front of her. "Guess what?"

"Who adopted Sunny."

"I don't care. Why did I lose?"

"This woman comes in looking like she'd inhaled rocket fumes and calls the kitten to her and the amazing thing is Sunny responds and starts purring. I'd never seen anything like it. I was positive the woman would scare her. But the kitten wasn't frightened."

Trent tapped the stem of his wine glass impatient. "So?"

"She was your doctor."

Trent frowned as the image of his GP came to mind. "Dr. Kohl? I thought she hated cats."

"No, the one you met at the wedding. She came in with a guy. A good looking guy. She looked really cozy with him. I think he was also at the wedding because he seems familiar too. Sorry." She motioned to the glass. "Drink up."

"You're sure it was her?"

"See for yourself." Mindy pulled out her cell phone. "They sent a picture of Sunny in her new home. It's amazing how quickly she's adjusted. She already has a favorite toy."

Trent looked at the photo and felt as if he'd been kicked in the gut. There she was again. Smiling. He remembered the sound of her laughter, which echoed in his mind. He felt oddly depressed. He couldn't believe he'd struck out so soon.

Mindy took a sip of her wine then set it down. "She saw your picture and didn't even mention you."

"I get it."

"Not even a hint."

He shot her a glance; she took another sip of her drink a smile tugging on her lips.

He sat back and folded his arms. "You're enjoying this."

"I told you I was right. You don't have to be anyone else to find the right woman. Now let's talk about your first date..."

ERIN STARED AT THE PHOTO OF TRENT WITH THE kitten. Brandon and Tara had decided to keep the name Sunny, which suited her. Should she call him and let him know that? She'd hoped that he would have been interested enough to call her first, but he hadn't. Was that a sign? *Ask a guy out* her brother had challenged her. It didn't matter if he said no. The attempt was all that counted. But she didn't want him to say no. She had looked him up and discovered he had co-founded SonTil Sounds. Why hadn't he told her that? Perhaps he was shy or humble, but he didn't seem that way.

She didn't have to call. She could just text him. What would she say? *Hi it's Erin. You might not remember me but we met at Dorothy and Derrick's wedding. You let me touch your birthmark.* No, that sounded wrong. Or she could say *Hi, it's Erin the ER doctor who asked about your scar.*

She shook her head. No that didn't sound right either. She wouldn't mention his scar or his birthmark or anything about his body although images of it had seeped into her dreams. Delicious dreams. But she would be polite and neutral. *Would you like to go out some time? My treat? Or does SonTil Sounds offer tours?*

Erin tossed her phone down on the couch. She was helpless. This was why she didn't ask guys out.

Her phone alerted her to a text. She saw Jeremiah's number. She cringed. She'd told him their relationship wasn't working and he was still determined to contact her. Before she could reply, the doorbell rang.

She opened the door and started to say, "What are you doing here?" but the tongue he shoved into her mouth stopped her. His arms circled her waist and pulled her close and she felt like she was being assaulted by a jellyfish. She pushed him away.

"I told you not to do that!"

Jeremiah grinned. "What's wrong with a guy trying to steal a kiss?"

She resisted the urge to wipe her mouth. That would be rude and she didn't want to hurt his feelings. "Try stealing something else." She took out her earrings. "Like my jewelry."

He laughed. "Have you eaten?"

"It's my day off."

"I know. Why do you think I'm here?"

She sighed. "We're not a good match. I don't want to waste your time."

"You're not." He planted another wet kiss on her lips before she could back away. "I think you're amusing."

"Amusing?"

He nodded. "You're a little uptight. But I like the

challenge of trying to loosen you up. If you did, you'd have a lot more fun. Caitlin could give you some lessons."

She wasn't surprised he remembered her cousin's name. She always left an impression. Erin gently pushed him out the door. "I'm seeing someone else."

"No, you're not."

"I think you should too. Caitlin's free. Enjoy."

She closed the door and ignored his knocking and texts. She wiped her mouth and stifled a scream. *Amusing? Uptight?* Anything would be better than another night with Jeremiah. Or someone similar. She was tired of falling for guys who seemed mysterious and interesting at first then either were vain or as emotionally deep as a bedpan.

She picked up her phone and typed a message to her brother. She needed his help for an idea. She didn't care if Trent turned her down. At least she would try for something better. She was finally breaking a pattern.

Trent watched Mindy go through her second glass of wine wondering how he could re-strategize and regain the advantage with Erin. He may not be her first choice, but he needed to at least be back in the running. How would Xavier handle this? He'd see it as a challenge. Trent definitely knew it was one. The sound of a group of happy frogs broke the silence, alerting him to a text message.

"Aren't you going to check your phone?" Mindy asked.

Trent absently looked at his cell phone then paused not quite sure what he was looking at. It showed a picture of the little black kitten dressed in scrubs with a photo of Erin and over it a message that said, "Coffee some time?"

"What are you looking at?" Mindy asked.

He began to grin. "I didn't lose."

"What?"

He showed her the screen.

"Aw...that is so cute."

"I know."

"How she got to dress up a cat like that I don't know." She squinted. "Or did she draw it on somehow?"

"Patient. I only had to be patient. I told you she'd contact me."

Mindy sat back and frowned. "You don't have to look so pleased with yourself."

"Why not? You were." He winked. "Don't worry, cuz. I'll accept a payment plan."

"You're going to love her and leave her?"

"That's the Brewster way." He raised his glass. "Let the games begin."

CHAPTER 13

Brandon opened the door to his sister's beaming face. "He said 'When?'," Erin said.

"What?" Brandon said a little groggy. He'd fallen asleep on the couch after a hearty dinner.

She came inside and closed the door behind her. "You know how I asked you to take a picture of Sunny and send it to me and you asked me why and I said I couldn't tell you yet?"

He nodded.

"Well, I used it to ask him out. The guy in the photo with the kitten." She paused. "Although I first met him at Derrick's wedding and—"

Brandon held up his hand. "Wait a minute. What are you talking about?"

"Is that you, Erin?" Tara called from the living room. "We have some extra curry chicken if you're interested."

"Yes, it's me," she replied, looking past Brandon. Her gaze fell to Sunny who was brushing against her leg. She bent down and stroked her. "And thank you but I've already eaten and I can't stay. I just wanted to tell Brandon something." She straightened and returned her gaze to him. "Can you believe it?"

"Believe what?"

"I asked a guy out to coffee and he said 'When?'. Look." She showed him the image on her cell phone.

He rubbed his eyes, wondering if he was still half-asleep. "It's a dog wearing headphones."

"It's *his* dog and he sent it in response to my picture of Sunny wearing scrubs." She turned the screen to face her. "It's amazing how much his dog looks like him. They have the same soulful, kind brown eyes."

Brandon affectionately rubbed her head. "I think you've been working too hard."

She lightly swatted his hand away. "I thought you'd be proud of me. I also broke up with Jeremiah."

"That deserves a hug." He gave her a quick embrace. "Bravo."

Her expression grew serious. "So you have to do your part and take the blame."

He bowed, unfazed by the consequences he would likely face. "With pleasure."

"Brandon," Tara said. "You shouldn't have her standing in the foyer like that. At least get her something to drink."

"No, really. I have to dash," Erin said, not wanting to get her brother into trouble. It was really important to Tara to treat visitors well, even family. And they both knew if she stayed a few more minutes Erin would be plied with grape juice and a plate filled with curried chicken and rice. Erin quickly kissed him on the cheek. "Thanks for this."

"I haven't done anything yet," he said oddly touched. He hadn't seen his sister this excited in a long time.

"You've done plenty. You forced me to change." She waved her cell phone. "I never would have asked a guy out like this before. I never would have thought to. I really think my luck has changed."

Brandon cleared his throat, suddenly worried about her optimism. Erin jumped into everything one hundred percent and he didn't know anything about this guy. "It's only coffee. Don't get ahead of yourself."

"No, he's different. I don't think he'll mistreat me or be like the rest. I've taken a chance and it's worked. Things are looking up." She opened the door just as Tara was walking towards her. She waved. "Talk to you later."

Brandon watched his sister leave. He felt a light hand on his back then his shoulder. "You look worried," Tara said.

He sighed and closed the door. "I shouldn't be."

Tara stood in front of him, her voice concerned. "What's going on?"

"She met someone. They're going out for coffee."

Tara frowned, confused. "And that's a bad thing?"

"No, she's happy. She thinks her luck has changed."

Tara smiled. "Maybe it has."

He nodded hoping they were both right.

CHAPTER 14

She was hooked.

Completely hooked.

The Xavier technique had worked and he planned to breakup with her that evening. He'd met his goal and won. A month had passed in the order he'd expected it to.

In less than two weeks Erin had agreed to be exclusive and had squeezed him into her busy schedule (a doctor's prized possession his parents hadn't easily altered from). And lately her days had been hectic, twice he'd seen bags under her eyes and told her she needed to pack a snack and drink to rehydrate (he knew most doctors were ignorant when it came to nutrition). The old Trent would have made sure to make her a homemade replenishment drink, delivered it to her apartment in the morning or at the hospital, depending on what was most convenient for her, that provided vitamin C, potassium with a little bit of magnesium and calcium that tasted great without a lot of added sugar, which was common with most popular sports drinks.

But the new Trent just gave her a link to a site where she could find out the information on her own. Erin had smiled and thanked him for caring. He'd shrugged in response but over the next week he had to stop himself from asking her if she'd checked the site yet, made one of the suggested drinks and had it helped. Despite himself, sometimes he worried about her burning herself out. She was the kind of woman who seemed to give everything one hundred and twenty percent and didn't look after herself (but that also wasn't unusual for doctors). Within three weeks she'd kissed him like a lover and cooked him dinner like a wife. She made no secret that she wanted to be with him every chance she got. She was fun, enthusiastic and wouldn't have given him the time of day before. He had to break up fast before he got resentful.

No other girlfriend had ever gone out of their way to impress him the way she did. The more distant he was— he was never moody, but reticent, quiet—the more she chatted and asked questions. The more inward he became, the harder she worked to please him. Guys like Xavier had it so easy. He'd proven he could be like him and it made him sick. He'd shown that all the effort he'd put into his previous relationships had been meaningless. Women didn't want guys who were helpful and considerate. They wanted to fawn over and worry about guys who really didn't give back much, if anything. He had to grit his teeth every time Erin apologized, worried that she'd offended him somehow. Fooling her had all been so easy, but then again, doctors were the easiest to fool as long as you stroked their ego.

Fortunately, he looked forward to giving Vince money for his summer school program, they'd put it to good use next year. Breaking up with her wouldn't be fun, but necessary in order to end this stupid game. He knew the carefree manner and way he'd say it. The thought made his palms sweat a little, he'd never broken up with someone before, but it was nice to be on the other end for once. But he'd do it his own way—Xavier either ignored calls, made sure he was seen with another woman, or sent a text. He couldn't go that far. He knew what he had to do. Then he'd focus on his business and forget about women at least for the next decade.

But before he broke up with Erin he had a job to do.

Trent parked outside the quaint building that housed Yardley's Antiques. Several weeks back he'd promised Vince he'd see what he could do about his aunt's store, not sure he could do much. He no longer did what he called sonic rebranding anymore.

Like the first seven notes of Disney's *When You Wish Upon a Star*, which reminded people of their childhood trips to the a forenamed theme park or the animated movie *Pinocchio*, he'd learned how to use the powerful sensory tool of sound to raise a story in someone's mind.

And the moment he'd entered the beautifully designed antiques store he knew why business was struggling. Despite what he saw (the antique cashier, the display cases, the expert lightning) or smelled (the worn wood, old books) the place *sounded* wrong.

The tempo of the classical music coming through the speakers was too fast, the store needed a more leisurely tempo selection to encourage people to stay and browse. The shop's front door was soundless; instead of a light swoosh of sound like someone entering an exciting cave of riches. Or he would encourage the sound of a light ringing of a bell and perhaps the soft creak of a hinge to encourage a memory—like the fizz sound a soda pop bottle makes when one twists the top—the floorboards were too harsh giving the sound of a concert hall instead of a cozy venue. With minor tweaks it would be a very robust business. He was disappointed when even the cash register didn't have an authentic sound and suggested a slight patter and ring sound when adding up customer's items.

He'd come on a return visit to see what changes, if any, had been made. He was pleasantly surprised when he opened the door and a tingling bell rang. The sounds of his shoes against the ground was more muted; a soft, lovely melody greeted him and in the distance he heard the ring of the antique cash register. But what was even better was the sound of people—the movement of bodies, the cadence of voices—the place was busy. He nodded at Willard Lee, husband of the owner. He was a dour looking Asian-American man, but gave him a brief grin of acknowledgement before he straightened the frame of an old map.

When Vince's aunt-in-law, Sally, saw Trent she rushed forward. He didn't know why but she always reminded him of a Victorian prostitute with her dramatic eye makeup against her Caucasian features, smoker's voice and tall frame. But the smile she gave him was as sweet as an angel. She ran the shop with her husband of thirty years and their twenty-three year old daughter, Cathy. It had been a new venture after many years of being, as she liked to call it "a cubicle slave" in an investment company. "What do you think?" she said in a low voice, and he felt his skin grow warm since she made those simple words sound like a come-on.

He cleared his throat and smiled. "The place sounds wonderful. You did a great job."

"We wouldn't have been able to do it without you. You're the one who told us which flooring to try and—"

Trent waved her praise away. "I only made suggestions. You did the hard work."

"Work is right. We're all still recovering. It's been exhausting. Cathy's been going almost non-stop. Missed a meal or two, but she was as excited as we were to see it all finished. We saw the effects of our changes almost right away." She winked. "Nothing beats the sound of the register tallying up an order and—"

The sound of something crashing to the ground in the storage room stopped her words.

"I'll see what it is," her husband said.

"It didn't sound like something expensive," Sally said trying to make light of the situation.

Then they heard Willard cry out and say, "Sally, come quick!"

For some reason when Trent followed Sally into the storage room he saw the blood first. Then Cathy's unconscious body on the ground with a knife sticking out of her arm.

He rushed forward. "She's still alive. No, don't pull it out!" he ordered when Willard reached to remove the knife. "Sally, stop screaming. She's breathing, her pulse is weak but it's still there." He looked at Willard. "Call an ambulance. Now."

CHAPTER 15

A crazy day.

Erin thought she'd get a chance to breathe before another crisis but she was wrong.

After finally convincing a father to let her sew up his daughter who'd suffered a facial dog bite. (He'd wanted a plastic surgeon but with patience he'd let her do her job) while a woman in another cubicle shouted at a nurse because she wanted her daughter seen to—now! And later attending to three anxious looking people who had been sitting outside the X-ray area wearing arm slings she had hoped for a moment of silence.

But the whirl of the ambulance siren in the distance and her charge nurse, Hector Ruiz, telling her of an unconscious young woman who had just arrived let her know there would be no calm in the storm.

"I can hardly get anything intelligible out of her," Hector said. He was an efficient, compact man with silvering, dark hair and an ability to put people at ease.

He expertly diverted resources where they were needed and usually was able to give her all the information she needed before she saw a patient. He made her job easier.

But when she saw the patient she could instantly see his problem. The mother sobbed over her daughter and every question she asked was met with gibberish. She was barely able to give them any information. "Is there anyone who could tell us what happened?"

"I'll see," Hector said then left. Moments later Trent entered.

Erin quickly recovered her surprise, pushed away all the unnecessary questions that instantly sprung to mind, "What are you doing here? How do you know them? Why do you look so pale and uneasy?" and said, "What happened?"

"I wasn't there when it happened. She was alone in the storage room when we heard the crash. That's all I can tell you."

"And she was fine before this?"

"Yes, she's very healthy."

"She didn't report feeling sick or dizzy?"

Trent walked over to the mother who was stroking her daughter's hand. "Sally? How was Cathy before? This morning did you suspect anything?" he said in a soft voice.

She mumbled something. He looked at Erin. "No, she was fine."

"Does she take any medications?"

"No."

"Had any recent illnesses?"

Trent gently spoke to the woman again. She vehemently shook her head. "No." He met her gaze. "And before you ask, no she isn't taking any nonprescription drugs either. She doesn't drink or smoke. And she's not seeing anyone."

"That you know of," Erin clarified, used to people keeping secrets from their families.

His tone hardened. "She doesn't."

Erin inwardly shrugged. She wouldn't argue with him. "Any change in her routine?"

"No, except—"

"What?"

"They've been doing extra work around the shop. They're all exhausted. Sally mentioned that Cathy had been working so hard that she's missed several meals, if that means anything."

"That could mean everything. Thanks."

It took some quick thinking but Erin was finally able to go with an instinct based on the symptoms. When the blood work came back she was certain she knew what to do.

***

DIABETES.

Trent never would have expected that to be the cause.

Cathy had suffered diabetic shock due to severe hypoglycemia and fainted, landing on the knife she'd been using to cut open a box, which, thankfully, struck the fatty part of her arm. She'd hit her head on a chair, resulting in a nasty gash on the side of her head, which had to be stitched up. Fortunately, she would be fine.

Trent wasn't sure her parents would be. The Lees sat in the hospital waiting room, Willard wiping his eyes and Sally shaking her head perplexed, while Erin explained that they would be able to see Cathy once she was placed in a room. They planned to keep her for observation overnight but were certain she'd be able to leave tomorrow.

Trent was eager to leave. The sounds of the emergency department accosted him—a softly crying child, the boisterous laughter of three older guys who smelled like booze, one with a blood soaked bandage wrapped around his arm; the sound of footsteps, impatient voices. But Erin seemed immune to it all as she leaned forward and gave the Lees her full attention. She remained steady, focused, in control. Outside the hospital she was always so bouncy and energetic, he hadn't expected to see this side of her.

And she looked damn sexy in her green scrubs. He swore. It was all an act. He'd been in enough hospitals to tell.

He could spot pretence a mile away; smell insincerity (his mother had perfected it), but strangely Erin had neither. At least he couldn't spot it yet. She was a master. For now every word, look and gesture appeared to be sincere. Her team also admired her. The charge nurse usually took cues from the doctor and Trent could clearly see that there was a true trust and respect between them.

But he could imagine her behind closed doors and

the cruel, callous comments she could make about her patients. He'd heard them all.

"But I don't understand," Sally said. "How can our daughter have diabetes? She's young and she's not over-weight. Wouldn't we have known if she'd had it since a child?"

Erin's voice was patient. "The onset of diabetes in adults can happen at any age and for many reasons. We'll have to do further tests to see what type she has. But what you need to know is that she will fully recover and with the right care will have a full vibrant life."

"Thank you. You've been so kind."

Don't fall for it. She's only doing her job. She's paid to look like she cares.

The Lees were notified that a room was free and they could see their daughter. "I'll wait here," Trent told them. He wanted to be as close to the exit as he could manage. They nodded and left.

Erin stayed behind and to his surprise reached out and covered his hand with hers. "I know it must all be such a shock seeing someone you care about like that. But she'll be fine."

He nodded, resigned. Even if it was all an act it would seem rather callous to breakup with her tonight. He'd give her another week then let her down easy.

"When does your shift end?"

She jumped to her feet. "I have three more hours."

It looked like they'd be a long three hours. She already looked worn. "Have you made one of those drinks, yet?"

Erin frowned. "Drinks?"

He slowly rose to his feet. "The ones to help rehy-drate you."

She grinned, for a moment resembling a naughty child who'd gotten caught doing something bad. "Not yet, sorry. But I will."

Trent shoved his hands into his pocket and gripped his hand into a fist. It wasn't something she should put off. "Fine."

The charge nurse came to her. "Doctor?"

"Got to go." She kissed him on the cheek. "Don't look so worried your friend will be fine."

Trent watched her disappear behind the large brown doors irritated that it wasn't Cathy he was truly worried about.

CHAPTER 16

The sound of laughter might swallow the screams.

Not that Trent thought that Erin would do that when he broke up with her but he wanted to be prepared for any possibility. (Xavier had once broken up with a girlfriend at one of their rare holiday family dinners. After she'd found another woman's naked photo on his phone, she'd screamed so loud Trent was certain all the glass in the house would shatter. They didn't.)

Trent had chosen not to take Erin to a restaurant or any other enclosed area where what was about to unfold could be amplified by walls. This park, only a couple miles away from her apartment complex, was perfect. In the distance they could hear children laughing on the playground, the pounding feet of joggers as they ran past. If she slapped him, shouted at him, or burst into tears the sound wouldn't echo but instead would be swallowed by the surrounding trees and the soft breeze drifting between them.

He had to do it today and stop stalling. He'd thought of doing it last week when they went to the sunflower garden, but she'd had too much fun and he thought the hour drive back would be awkward. This way Erin could storm away from him and safely get back home either by walking, hailing a lift or riding a bus. He knew Xavier wouldn't have thought of these things, but Trent couldn't help himself. The bet was over. He'd already collected his money from Mindy and given the money to Vince without telling him how he'd gotten it. It was time to end it.

Quick, easy, as painless as possible. They sat together under the shade of an oak tree on a soft blue checkered blanket with the remnants of their picnic tucked away in the cooler Erin had brought with her and a large back-pack. She watched a couple walking their two cocker spaniels and Trent briefly wondered if she was imagining what would happen if one of the dogs got lose and attacked someone. He took a deep breath, now was the best time to get it over with.

"Erin—"

She jumped, startled out of her thoughts. "Oh, sorry. Did you say something?"

"No." He cleared this throat. "The thing is—"

She held up her hand. "Wait, before I forget." She grabbed her backpack, unzipped it and pulled out a book. "Here."

He took the book and read the title: *The Quick and Easy Way to Understanding Type 1 Diabetes*. He also noticed a pink sticky note on top with a name and phone number.

"What is this?" he asked.

"It's for Cathy. A good endocrinologist can be very hard to find." She tapped the note. "So I asked around and got this referral. She may find it even more difficult to get a good primary care who understands her situation, but it's not impossible."

He frowned confused. "What are you talking about?"

"Cathy," Erin said sending him a strange look. "Your friend. The one who was in the emergency room about a week ago."

He nodded. "Right."

"I got this book that should help her and her parents understand what she has. It can be very overwhelming. And make sure she gets in touch with this doctor. I don't know everything, but if they have questions they can feel free to call me."

Trent stared at the book and the note. "But why did you do this?"

"Because I thought it might be helpful. How is she by the way?"

He stared at the book amazed. "Who?"

"Cathy." Erin sighed with frustration. "What is with you today? I want to know how she and her parents are doing. They received quite a shock."

He paused not sure he'd heard correctly. He slowly lifted his head. "You're asking about Cathy and her parents?"

"Yes."

"You want to know how they're doing and you want me to give them this book and referral?"

"Yes."

"Why?"

Erin blinked, confused. "Why wouldn't I? I was her doctor, remember?" Her gaze grew intense. "Are you sure you're feeling all right?"

"I'm perfectly fine. But I don't understand why you're asking about a situation that's over. You did your job. The patient is well. What more is there?"

Erin stared at him shocked. "I don't know what to say to such a cold statement. Why wouldn't I care? She's not some widget I tweak a little and then send back into the world. She's a person with feelings and so are her parents. I'm very aware of the impact a visit to the ER can have on someone, especially when they're given news that will change their lives. No, I don't get paid for it, but I don't shut off my mind and heart when I'm off the clock. I became a doctor because I want to help and I care. Why are you looking at me like that?"

Because he couldn't believe it. He felt as if his world was suddenly spinning off its axis. On her day off, she was asking about a patient? In her spare time she'd made inquiries and bought a book for her? She cared how Cathy was doing? Really?

A cold dread spread through his stomach. Erin was the real deal. Something he'd never met before. Something he never thought existed: A true caring doctor.

Doctors are kind. At five he'd laughed at the statement. He didn't believe it. He knew it wasn't true. But he couldn't laugh now. Erin was who the librarian had been talking about. In a noisy, fast paced environment, Erin had taken her time with Cathy and the Lees. She didn't chide Sally for her behavior or mock Willard's tears; she didn't treat Cathy like one of many. She had treated her like a person who mattered. As if she would take special care of her and she did.

Erin was a truly, empathetic doctor. It was like meeting a unicorn. Something he'd only heard about in stories. If he hadn't seen it with his own eyes he wouldn't have believed it.

Within minutes she wasn't just a pretty doctor with a short afro and effusive grin. She was beautiful to him. Stunningly beautiful. All the time he'd been with her he'd never noticed the slight dimple in her cheek, the full form of her lips and her eyes. He'd always thought them bright, but now...now they were extraordinary. And he looked at her lips again and he wanted to kiss them, not as he had before—perfunctory, practiced—but with wild abandon. He wanted to feel the soft give of her breasts against his chest, the touch of her hands on his skin. He wanted...her. Completely.

That meant trouble.

He could feel himself falling and he couldn't stop himself.

He gritted his teeth.

He couldn't fall for a doctor.

He made a vow.

He feared he was going to break it.

Erin scrambled to her knees, grabbed his chin and forced him to look at her. "You're really beginning to scare me. What's going on? How do you feel right now?

Do you feel faint? Don't be shy with me. Tell me the symptoms."

Yes, he felt faint, dizzy, queasy. He felt his world was spinning and he didn't know how to stop it. *Yes, you do,* a tiny voice said. It sounded suspiciously like his brother. *Do what you came here to do. Break up with her before it's too late.*

He closed his eyes. "I'm fine. It's...just when I remember how we found her. It still gets to me."

He waited for a reply. He didn't hear her move. He wondered if he'd broken his cover. Xavier wouldn't have said something like that. It made him sound weak. Fine, it had to end anyway. He opened his eyes and saw Erin looking at him, her sweet, brown gaze glistening with tears. His heart constricted.

"You don't have to be embarrassed by how much you care about her. Please don't be shy with me. I know how much you worried that day. I saw it." She opened her bag again and pulled out another book called *A Quick Guide to Type 1 Diabetes.* "I thought we could go through this together."

He cleared his throat, touched. "Thanks."

She tilted her head. "But something is still bothering you. Wasn't there something you wanted to tell me?"

I'm not who you think I am. He shook his head. "No."

"Good. One more thing."

"Another book?" he wondered aloud as she rifle through her backpack.

"No, this is for Roger." She placed a medium sized red box on the blanket.

"What is that?"

"Sunny wanted to give Roger a gift."

"How did you know he'd found her?"

Erin frowned. "I didn't. I thought you did. That's what the write-up said."

Trent swore. Of course she wouldn't know the full story. He never let Mindy post that. He had to get his mind back in order.

"Roger found her?"

Trent opened the box. *Ignore the topic and she might drop the subject.* "Why would she send him a gift?"

"She noticed the stuffed toys in the background of the photo you sent me and thought he might like another one."

Trent listened to the squawk of a blue jay high up in a tree. The day was getting worse. Not only was she a caring doctor, she truly was a sweet and affectionate girl-friend. Few people paid attention to his brown Lab's scavenger collection.

Erin leaned forward, close enough that when she spoke her warm breath fanned his skin. "Now tell me what happened."

He sighed. He could redirect her, continue to ignore her, but he wasn't in the mood. "You can't tell anyone."

"I won't."

"Roger found her on a walk. He alerted me to her."

Erin rested her chin in her hand. "I knew it. There's a deep, soulful look in his eyes. The eyes of a rescuer. Like you."

"I don't rescue. I only follow the dog when he gets that look."

Her eyebrows shot up. "He's done it before?"

Trent swore again. What was wrong with him today? Why did she keep making him reveal things he shouldn't? "No."

"Liar." She snatched the box back.

"Hey!"

"I'm going to give this to him myself. How come you haven't introduced us yet?"

"Because he's shy and he doesn't like a lot of questions. He won't tell you anything."

"I can handle shy. And I'm good at keeping secrets." She pressed her hands together. "Please let me meet him."

Meeting Roger would mean her coming by his place. She'd never seen his place before. He'd orchestrated it that way. His place was still like the old Trent. But if he wanted to get to know her better...

A month wasn't enough. He needed more time.

A lot more time.

He motioned her closer.

"What?"

He didn't want to talk anymore. He didn't want to think anymore. "I'm going to kiss you," he whispered, then did.

CHAPTER 17

He'd never kissed her like this before.

His lips had always felt warm and spicy-sweet on hers, but this was divine ecstasy. This was a knee weakening, blood pounding, hot, deep kiss.

If she'd known that giving Trent a book would make him act like this she would have done it a lot sooner. He was still a mystery to her. Not always in the way she would hope. At times she wished she knew, rather than guessed, that he was happy with her. He kept his emotions so guarded. There had been times when she suspected that he wasn't as serious about their relationship as she was, but every time she began to question herself—or him—he would surprise her with a funny text or call her up and ask her how she was doing.

Those moments made her feel unsure. Perhaps she was expecting too much too soon. Not giving him enough time to feel more at ease with her. It was only at the hospital that he seemed the most human to her. She'd seen shock, worry, anger, confusion cross his features, but, most of all, she'd seen tenderness in the way he'd held Mrs. Lee and gently spoken to her.

For a moment she didn't recognize him. There was something different about him. Not exactly vulnerable, but incredibly sensitive. She'd briefly been jealous of the older woman, wondering if he'd ever speak to her that way, before she pushed the thought from her mind.

Perhaps that's why he protected himself so much. When he put the mask away (Was it a mask or how he really was?) he appeared to be someone else. Someone more approachable. Someone she wanted to know. She felt guilty for seeing fault in him. She did like to be with him and he was such a refreshing change to all the other men she'd been with. But sometimes she wished that she felt a little more special with him. That he didn't act like he could be somewhere else having just as good a time.

Or maybe that was her own insecurities rising up. It wasn't a man's job to make a woman feel special, she was supposed to feel that in her own right. She shouldn't feel annoyed that she was almost always the one planning their dates, scheduling their meetings. He showed up. Wasn't that enough? And he was a great kisser. He was polite. Well mannered. A great kisser (yes, she'd already mentioned that but it mattered). However, he didn't seem interested in taking their relationship any further than that. She wasn't too disappointed, she wasn't sure if she was ready yet. There were moments when she still felt shy and awkward with him.

She doubted having sex with him would make it any

easier. Not that she didn't want to. She fantasized about it—slowly taking off his clothes, touching her tongue to his warm, brown skin—but always stopped herself before the actual act.

She felt unnerved by him and not always in a good way. Since she couldn't always read how he felt about something when he was standing up and clothed, how would she be able to gauge him when they were naked in each other's arms? She doubted he would be open to her asking him a series of questions like "Do you like that?" "How is this position for you?" "Are you ready to come?"

No, that would be disastrous.

But this kiss made her wonder. There was no denying how he felt about her now. It both aroused and frightened her. He wasn't acting like himself. She drew away.

He licked his lips and stared at her mouth like a hungry man at a buffet. Her pulse quickened as her skin grew warm. "Trent?"

He didn't lift his gaze, when he spoke his voice was deeper than she'd ever heard it before. "What?"

"What was that for?"

He lowered his gaze.

"Trent?"

"Do I need a reason?"

"No, but—"

He kissed her again and she enjoyed it, but she didn't feel safe. She didn't trust her feelings for him. She didn't know what part was the real Trent and the part she wanted him to be. He still had kind eyes. But he rarely smiled; when he did it was brief, fleeting. And she hadn't met the handsome, sweet looking guy in the photo holding up Sunny. Until now. She'd seen a slight glimpse when he'd held the book in his hand and then when he mentioned Roger, before something came over his features again. Was it so bad to share with her that his dog liked to find strays? That he cared about Cathy and her family? How did he know them? How long? Did everything have to be a mystery with him?

Then again, she had to give him space. Her brother had warned her about asking too many questions and she didn't want to scare him away. She hoped by going through the book with him he would open up and trust her a little bit more.

She pushed him away and gasped, feeling hot and breathless. "No more kisses."

"Why not?"

"Not until I meet Roger."

He hesitated and that worried her. What was the reluctance? What was he hiding?

He studied her intently and she held her breath. "Are you sure you want to?" he finally asked.

"Definitely."

He released a long breath as if coming to a major decision. "Then I'll make it happen."

CHAPTER 18

He was sinking deeper and deeper and loved every minute.

Trent tossed a package of dates and dried apricots in his cart as he pushed his way through the produce section of the global market he liked to frequent. The sounds of a Spanish ballad floated through the speakers as he passed through a selection of dragon fruit, taro root and roasted shelled peanuts. Beside him two men argued in Portuguese near the avocadoes while a young couple looked at a large aloe vera stalk. The man held a baby who reached out to touch it and the mother quickly pushed the baby's hand away.

Trent couldn't stop a smile, briefly imagining himself as the father and Erin as the mother. She wouldn't keep the aloe out of reach. She'd likely buy it so that the child could run its chubby, little fingers over the pointy edges and smooth center. And he could imagine kneeling in front of his son or daughter and using the aloe vera gel to cover a cut or bruised kneecap or elbow they'd managed to get while playing. And their tears would turn into smiles. He'd use the remainder of the stalk in a drink for Erin to get her through a hectic day. She'd smile at him, kiss him when she returned home (her day started too early for him to see her) and they'd spend the evening taking Roger on a walk under a clear spring sky.

His family.

The desire to make the image real, shocked him in its ferocity. He knew what he wanted, but hadn't realized how much until now. He would make a good husband and father. He pushed the idea down. It would happen one day, just not yet. For now he had a relationship he wanted to keep. Nurture. Grow. He wondered if Erin knew about the market and whether she'd like to go shopping with him one day.

Not unless you want to lose face, he could hear his brother say. His brother and father barely knew what the inside of a grocery store looked like. The ladies in their lives always took care of that detail or ordered in. Trent sighed. It was a secret pleasure he'd keep to himself for now. He'd let Erin know about the market but would never suggest going with her no matter how much he wanted to.

"You don't like dates," a familiar voice said. "And what is up with your clothes?"

Trent turned and saw Mindy giving him the once over. She was used to seeing him in corduroys or jeans and T-shirts not the tan tailored jacket and dark trousers he was wearing. She probably also noticed the haircut.

He shrugged, hoping to appear nonchalant. "I'm trying something new."

She lifted the package of dates. "And these? Don't tell me you've suddenly gotten a taste for them."

"No."

"Did they fall in your cart by mistake?"

Trent took the bag from her and set it back in the cart. "No."

"Then why are you buying them?"

He bit his lip, wondering if he should tell her the truth. She would likely find out anyway. He pushed his cart towards the dairy section. "Erin likes them."

Mindy jumped in front of his cart and stared at him. "You're still seeing her?"

He reached for a block of feta cheese. "Hmm."

"But it's been nearly two months!"

"Hmm."

"You were supposed to break up with her over a month ago."

"Hmm."

Mindy hit his arm. "Stop pretending this isn't a big deal." She looked him up and down with renewed interest. "Is this why you're dressed like that? I hardly recognized you. Are you really keeping this farce up?"

He placed the cheese in his cart. "It's working."

Mindy threw her hands in the air. "Have you lost your mind? What are you doing? I paid you the money. You won. You were supposed to break up with her and move on."

Trent turned and headed down the produce section again. "I didn't want to."

"Why not?"

"Why do you think?"

"You like her and you're using her. Just like Xavier. Does Ana know about this?"

Trent tensed at the mention of his sister's name. "Why would she?"

"Have you spoken to her recently?"

He sighed, wondering when he'd be able to talk to his sister again without a lingering sense of pain. It had been months since their last conversation. "I will."

Mindy stared at him for a long moment. "You're probably too busy right now. Congratulations, you're really becoming a true ass—"

Trent paused, gripped the handle of his cart and said through clenched his teeth, "She likes me like this and I don't want to lose her."

"If she likes guys like this, you're going to lose her anyway once she discovers what you're really like. Break up with her. Now."

He grabbed a zucchini. "No."

"You're taking this too far."

He put the zucchini back. "It's only been two months. It's not a big deal." He took Mindy's shoulders, turned her in another direction and gave her a light shove before he muttered, "I have to buy bug spray."

Mindy turned back to him. "It won't help. I'm not going anywhere and you can't say your relationship's not a big deal. With you everything is a big deal."

Trent shook his head. "It will all be fine. I went to Xavier for advice and—"

Mindy's eyebrows shot up, her voice cracked in surprise. "Xavier! You went to Xavier for advice?"

Trent looked around embarrassed. "Keep your voice down."

She grabbed her forehead. "I don't believe you're doing this."

"It's working."

"Trent," Mindy said, lowering her voice to a soft, understanding tone. "I know you've been hurt in the past, but to use a woman this way—"

"Stop saying that. I'm not using her."

"That's what your brother does. Or didn't he tell you that?"

"The women don't complain."

Mindy shook her head. "I can't believe you went to Xavier to get advice on women."

"Why not? He's gotten me this far."

Mindy folded her arms. "Is it because she's a doctor? Is this some sort of perverse revenge because you hate doctors so much?"

He walked away.

"Yes, that's pure Xavier too," she called after him. "Avoid the topic."

Trent turned sharply to her, his gaze hard. "This is my last warning. Keep your voice down."

Mindy adjusted her tone but not her disgust. "The old Trent would have the decency to answer my question. The guts too."

Trent sighed. "I'm not going back to how my life was before. Erin likes me, cares about me. I've never had..." He took a deep breath. "This means a lot to me. Maybe I am being selfish, but I want this and I'm not going to let it go."

Mindy sighed, resigned. "Fine. Who am I to stop you using the potent, effective Xavier technique on an unsuspecting victim?"

Trent shook his head. "Erin's not a victim and I only went to him for some tips. Don't make me feel guilty. She's happy with me the way I am." He glanced down when he heard the sound of thunder then rain. He briefly glanced at his phone and saw Dorothy's number. He'd been avoiding her calls since she'd returned from her honeymoon. He put the cell phone away.

"She doesn't know who you are."

Trent tapped his chest. "This is who I am."

Mindy touched the hem of his expensive jacket. "A guy who lies to her."

"I'm not lying. Much," he added when she sent him a stern look.

She curled her lip in disgust. "So you went to your wise older brother. Did he help you?"

More than expected, but Trent didn't want to delve into details. His brother had invited him over when Trent had called him up asking for advice without being specific. When he'd arrived at his brother's condo, a beautiful woman with dark skin and reddish brown hair, wearing an elegant red slip dress, had greeted him at the door. "Your brother will be out in a minute," she said in a soft cultured tone. "I've got some snacks in the dining room if you want to wait there."

"Thanks." Trent followed her into the dining room

and gawked at the elaborate spread—crab toast, stuffed olives, herbed squash spread on crostini.

"Are you expecting someone else?"

"No," his brother said coming into the room. He pulled out a chair and sat. "She likes to cook."

"It looks amazing."

"Thanks," she said. "Would you like anything to drink?"

"I'm fine for now, thanks."

She touched Xavier's shoulder. "What about you?"

He lifted her hand and kissed it. "Just leave us alone for a bit, love."

She nodded then left.

Trent watched her go. "How come she looks familiar?"

Xavier filled up his plate. "Spring 2016."

Trent shook his head. His brother was the only man he knew who referred to his women by the season and the year. Most women didn't last longer than a season. "Getting nostalgic?"

Xavier flashed a roguish grin. "No, she's trying to win me back." He winked. "Trying real hard."

Trent eyed the selection of food. "It shows."

Xavier waved his finger. "No, this isn't it. This is just a bonus."

Trent frowned. "I don't understand. What is she doing?"

"Everything." Xavier picked up a crab toast. "Sex with an ex is the best. Especially when they want you back. You should try it some time."

Trent rubbed his neck, his raised scar scratching his

palm. They both knew he'd never had an ex who wanted him back. But his luck had changed. He didn't plan to have another ex. He wanted Erin. "I'm seeing someone."

"Finally," Xavier said, sounding relieved. "Tell me it's not serious. The problem with you is you get serious too fast."

"If I could, I'd marry her."

Xavier closed his eyes as if in pain. "That's exactly what I mean."

"But I can't, so I want to keep her as long as I can."

Xavier stared at him. "Why can't you marry her?"

"It's a long story."

"Is she married?"

"No."

"Afraid she'll turn you down?"

"I didn't come here for counseling. I came for advice."

Xavier leaned back and shook his head. "You won't listen to my advice."

"Just tell me what you'd do in my shoes."

"I've never been in your shoes." He rested a hand on his chest. "Do I look like I want to be tied down?"

"Just pretend."

"Forced to eat one meal for the rest of my life?"

"Xavier."

He sighed, resigned and shook his head in pity. "What is she like? Professional?"

"She's an ER doctor at Treeline Hospital."

Xavier looked at him for a long minute then threw his head back and burst into laughter. He pointed at Trent his eyes dancing with amusement. "You had me there for a minute. I thought you were serious. Okay, why did you really want to see me?"

"I am being serious."

Xavier's humor turned into shock. "You're dating a doctor?"

Trent nodded.

Xavier started to stand. "I think I might need a drink after all."

"The fact that I'm seeing a doctor isn't the point. I'm trying to change. I don't want the relationships I've had in the past. I really like her and I want to keep her."

Xavier studied him for a moment as if processing Trent's words then said, "Does she know that?"

"Not in so many words."

He nodded pleased. "Good. Keep her guessing. Keep her a little off-balance. That keeps the relationship interesting. Don't ever let her really know how you feel. I've told you this before."

"She wants to see my place."

Xavier gave a low whistle.

"That bad, huh?"

"You bought a house in the suburbs. With an elementary school within walking distance. And isn't there a park close by too?"

"Yes, but—"

"What do you think that says?"

"Since I don't plan to move, what else can I do?"

"You'd need to make some changes."

"I know. Tell me what to do."

Xavier studied him. "You like her this much?"

He nodded.

"More than Dorothy?"

Trent steepled his fingers together. "I'm over her and want a new life."

"Completely new?"

"Yes."

"Then we'll also have to work on your wardrobe."

"Whatever it takes."

"I look forward to meeting this woman. There's a new club opening up. I can get you in."

"I'm game."

Xavier's smile widened. "That's what I like to hear."

And Xavier had turned Trent's place into a sophisticated bachelor pad. At least the places a guest would see. "Keep her out of the basement and close the other rooms. Make the main focus the living room, the kitchen and bedroom," his brother instructed him. He removed most of Trent's kitchenware telling him they made him look "too domestic"; hid all of Roger's toys and treasures because they made him look "soft" and replaced most of Trent's posters and statues with what Xavier deemed more modern items. The one area where Trent resisted his brother was the removal of two photos. One he had framed on his bookshelf and another was a magnet photo he had stuck on his fridge.

"No, pictures of Maya," Xavier said, taking them down.

"No one's going to notice."

Xavier sent him a stern look. "A woman would notice this and then you'd have to explain."

"So what? You may have gotten over it, but I haven't."

Xavier nodded. "That's your problem. You still choke

up when you talk about her. If you want this to work, you'll do as I say."

Putting Maya's photo away felt like losing her all over again, but he knew his brother was right. It would reveal too much about him, and Erin would ask a series of questions he didn't want to answer. His past needed to remain off limits.

After the house was organized, Xavier then selected a wardrobe for Trent to appear like a man with lots of money and women.

Mindy looked stunned after Trent told her what he'd done. "I'm almost afraid to see your place. Did you get rid of Roger?"

"Of course not."

"I'm not sure how far you'll go with this."

"It's not that bad."

Mindy looked at his clothes in dismay. "But this isn't you at all."

"It is me," Trent said wanting desperately for it to be true, although he secretly knew it wasn't. "It's the new me." And he'd take it as far as he needed to.

CHAPTER 19

Of all the things Erin had imagined to see that late summer evening with Trent, she hadn't imagined seeing him kissing another woman. But he was.

She couldn't believe it at first. Everything about the evening had felt a little surreal. At first, when they entered the new club with its stylish chrome décor and open modernist atmosphere she'd been surprised by Trent's selection. While visually stunning, every sound inside the club seemed to clash into each other, from the booming beat from the DJ to the voices on the upper floor. She would have thought a sound engineer would have found such an atmosphere painful, but Trent didn't seem to care as they were ushered to an exclusive table.

Erin didn't even try to imagine what it cost but he didn't seem the kind of man who worried about money. Tonight he wore a gorgeous black tailored suit that fit him beautifully and she wasn't the only woman to notice. He moved with a confident grace, as if he expected to turn heads, making her feel a little out of her element. She wasn't shy—she'd chosen a gold dress and long dangling earrings to make sure she didn't fade into the background —and she didn't mind the feminine attention he garnered —she was used to that from the other men she'd dated in the past. But she'd expected more.

She didn't want to admit that she was disappointed. The club, the clothes, Trent's walk was so...predictable. For one horrible moment she was reminded of a similar night out with Jeremiah. He'd flashed a credit card and gotten them a private table too. He'd relished the attention he'd received from both men and women. He'd been in his element. Like Trent. And again she got a gnawing suspicion that she didn't know Trent as well as she should have.

She slid into the booth fearing a typical evening where she had to feign being impressed with the exclusive table, the drinks and the food. She'd smile, even when she didn't feel like it and dance, waiting for the evening to end.

But Trent surprised her when he slid beside her and rested his arm behind her head as if he were staking claim. It was a gesture no man had ever done before and for a moment she was shocked then thrilled. She glanced at him and realized he was looking at the other women, but she also noticed that he looked at every man who seemed to take a quick glance at her quietly, but effectively, telling them she was his.

It gave her goose bumps and also made her feel more relaxed. Before that moment she'd felt like a wound up toy ready to burst on the dance floor and drink the night away. But the light touch of his fingers against the back of her neck; the heady scent of him eased any tension and made her feel calm.

She felt her heart leap with a renewed anticipation, when they ordered drinks. Perhaps the night would be better than she thought. But the mood between them changed when a lighter, sexy more predatory version of Trent approached the table. They shared a look and Trent quickly removed his arm and distanced himself a little.

"Xavier, this is Erin," Trent said.

Erin noticed the man's gaze heated when he shook her hand. He was just the type she would have dated in the past. Cultured, self-assured, selfish. "A pleasure to meet you," she said.

"Likewise."

A waitress in a tight dress with the club logo approached the table. Xavier motioned her away. "I'm not ready yet."

She nodded and left.

"Are you here alone?" Trent asked.

He nodded. "Seasons change fast."

Erin was prepared to ask Xavier how he'd learned about the club when an attractive woman wearing a form-fitting black dress and curly dark hair at the bar caught Trent's eye. "Excuse me," he said then joined her.

Erin watched him go, surprised that his typical walk was more hurried than his usual casual confidence. Was he that eager to see her?

"He's popular with the ladies," Xavier said as if reading her thoughts.

"No, surprise," Erin said, trying her best to act like she didn't care.

"He's just reuniting with an old friend," Xavier said.

That's when she saw them kiss. Not a light kiss. Not a kiss on the cheek or the brush of the lips. But a full, deep kiss

"Looks like a happy reunion," Xavier said with a laugh. "No need to get jealous. She's not the first one who wants him back."

Erin didn't know whether she wanted to cry or laugh. No need to be jealous? But she *was* jealous. Hugely jealous. She now could imagine how Trent got that large scar in a bar. She could picture an outraged ex coming at him with fury screaming "How dare you treat me this way!" before scarring him for life. She could picture him grabbing his neck to stop the bleeding, but he wouldn't deserve a doctor. He deserved to suffer a little.

But as she watched the kiss continue, Erin's anger turned to hurt. Trent didn't push the woman away. He didn't turn to look towards her with a guilty expression. He enjoyed it. Every second. She'd gotten it wrong again. She couldn't believe she'd gone out with a man who'd forgotten she was there. It was demoralizing. Trent was only a softer version of the type of man she'd dated before.

She'd changed her pattern, but not her luck. In Trent she'd seen what she'd wanted to see. He was no different than the rest. She'd been fooled by what she'd thought were kind eyes, pictures with kittens, the care he had for his friends.

But he didn't care about her. Not in the same way. He hadn't called her or contacted her first because he hadn't been that interested and now she had proof.

She looked down at her dress through eyes blurred by tears. She'd gone through all this work for nothing. She knew there would always be prettier, smarter women out there, but she'd thought she'd finally met someone who didn't care. Someone who truly liked her.

"Excuse me," she said, standing.

"Don't get upset," Xavier said. "It's nothing and you'll only look like a fool."

Erin smiled without humor. "Which is exactly what I am."

***

THE KISS HAD BEEN UNEXPECTED, BUT SO HAD BEEN the sight of Carlene at the bar. He'd hurried over to her to avoid a situation. He didn't want Erin to meet her because Carlene knew too much about the old Trent and could ruin everything. He wanted to say "hello" first and make sure to keep her away. But she'd looked at him said "Oh my God" and then kissed him.

The old Trent would have pulled away immediately, told her he was with someone else, but the new Trent heard his brother's voice in his head. *Be cool. Nothing wrong with flirting and women like to know that other women find their man attractive. You can use this to your advantage.* So he'd let her kiss him a little longer than he would have before he drew way. He grinned. "Nice to see you too."

She let her gaze trail the length of him. "What happened to you? You look amazing."

"Thanks, you do too. Where's uh..." He let his words trail off as if he'd forgotten the other man's name. Although his mind screamed it. Harold. Harold the accountant you dumped me for.

Carlene made a dismissive gesture with her hand. "Oh, he's long gone. Didn't I tell you? I was sure I sent you a text. Anyway, I realized I didn't really need excitement. That it can be exhausting, especially with two kids. But enough about me. Would you like—"

"I'm here with someone." Oh, how good that sounded.

Carlene looked disappointed, but not surprised. "Figures. But in case it doesn't work out, feel free to call. You know how to reach me. I'm in the area for now."

She winked then walked away and Trent briefly thought about what Xavier had told him about sex with an ex. He knew Carlene would be incredible in bed. But he was over her now. He felt triumphant with power. Handling women was so easy now. Carlene wanted him back. Even Dorothy had been texting him more than she ever did when they were a couple.

"You're so busy now," she'd told him when he'd stopped by her place last week to help her with a speaker issue that neither she nor Derrick could fix. He'd been tempted to tell her to call a professional, but he saw it as a test. He didn't want to avoid her. If he was going to get over her hold over him, he had to face every painful truth.

He had to drive up the brick driveway to their colonial home in an eyebrow raising zip code. He had to walk past the row of trimmed bushes and up the stone steps. He had to listen to the sound of his footsteps on the dark wood flooring in the expansive living room where in the evenings Dorothy and Derrick likely sat in front of a large flat screen TV with a built in fireplace to their left.

And he had to smell the scent of violets as she peeked over his shoulder to see his progress with the equipment. Every tiny torment was good for him. He had to remind himself why he could never go back to who he had been.

He quickly adjusted the crossed wires and got the speakers working again; pleased he'd been able to disappear before Derrick returned home from work. He could only take so much. However, he was surprised the speaker problem had been such an easy fix. He almost thought Dorothy had made it up just to have him come over, but that didn't make any sense. Why would she go through that much trouble just to see him?

"Trent?" Dorothy said as he stood from his crouched position where she'd hidden the speakers inside the sleek black entertainment unit.

"What?"

"I asked you what's kept you so busy. Are you working on a new project?"

Sort of. "Yes." He headed for the door.

"Really? What?"

He paused. She'd never asked him that before. She'd never been interested. It wasn't until that moment that he realized she was curious about him. Curious about what he was doing. He inwardly groaned. His father and brother were right, the more you ignored a woman the more they were interested in you. His new hypothesis was becoming depressingly predictable.

"I've got to go."

"We should get together some time."

He opened the door. "Sure."

She followed him down the stairs in her bare feet. "And if you're not seeing anyone—"

Trent opened his car. "I am."

She blinked. "You are? Who?"

He smiled. She was curious again. Part of it was annoying, but it also felt good. "You'll find out."

But Trent knew it wouldn't be any time soon. Dorothy was dangerous to his relationship with Erin. He'd have to be strategic.

Trent drummed his fingers on the bar at the memory. Tonight he'd avoided a possible disaster with Carlene, gotten his ego stroked in a way he could have only dreamed about in the past and now it was time to return to Erin.

But she wasn't at the table.

"Where is she?"

"Who?" Xavier said in a distracted voice as he stared into the sultry eyes of a new companion with hot red lips and long dark hair.

"Erin. Where is she?"

"She left."

Trent slid into his seat. "For the ladies' room?"

"No, for good."

He jumped to his feet. "And you let her go?"

"It's not my job to hold onto your women. She saw

you with the..." He snapped his fingers in an absent way. "What year was she again?"

Trent's heart raced. This was going all wrong. "I've got to find her and explain that—"

In one smooth motion, Xavier detangled himself from his new companion, grabbed his brother's arm and forced him to sit back down. "Don't go running after her." He turned to the woman at his side. "Sorry about this," he said politely, but his tone said "This is a private matter so your time is up." She shrugged unconcerned and left the table.

Trent struggled to pull his arm free. "Why shouldn't I go after her?"

"Because you cannot handle a woman like that," Xavier warned in a low voice. "You are no match for her. She'll have your balls in a handbag. Your scrotum in a—"

"No she won't." He became still and pinned his brother with a look. "Let me go or I will pound your face into the table."

Xavier released him, taking the threat seriously. "You're on dangerous ground. I've seen her type. I know her type." A quick grin touched the corner of his lips. "And if I'm honest, I like her type. But not you. I won't let you get involved with someone like her. You can't—"

Trent stood. "You don't understand. She's not what you think. She needs me. She needs someone to look out for her."

Xavier also rose to his feet. "Now you're embarrassing me and yourself. Shut up and look around you. In minutes you could have a beautiful, willing woman to take home tonight. Tonight! And if not here, somewhere else. Let her go and move on."

"I don't want anyone else."

"And that's why you always lose. You're making her too important. In a relationship you either look after her or she looks after you. There's no in-between. Become soft again and she'll treat you like all the rest. Like a dishrag."

Trent knew his brother's words were right. By going after Erin he was losing his edge. He wouldn't be the one in control. But he couldn't pretend that he wasn't worried. He walked away from the booth. "I at least have to make sure she's okay." *That she's safe. That she's not out wandering the night streets alone feeling angry and betrayed.* She was vulnerable and could be targeted. He wouldn't let that happen.

Xavier shook his head in pity. "You're making a mistake." He pointed at him. "Don't say I didn't warn you."

CHAPTER 20

Trent headed for the back exit, hoping he could find Erin before she left. He imagined her calling a ride, possibly in tears. He hoped she wasn't crying. He'd hate the thought that he'd made her cry. Maybe she'd slap him and call him names. He could take it. He would...

Trent stopped just yards away from the exit when he saw a flash of gold. He turned and saw Erin laughing with a guy. He didn't realize he was gripping his hand into a fist until he felt his nails biting into his palm. All worry left him like a swift breeze and in its place was a cauldron of anger. Not towards her, but him. This man. This man who dared to smile and touch the shoulder of his woman.

He'd never felt the teeth of jealousy engulf him like that before. Even at Dorothy's wedding he'd felt pain, not fury. And the thought of Erin in a wedding dress exchanging vows with someone else became too much to bare. *Oh hell no.* She was *his* and no man was going to take his place until he was ready to let her go.

He stormed up to the pair, took Erin's hand and said to the man, "Excuse me," amazed he could manage the words.

But his grip wasn't solid enough and Erin managed to pull her hand free. "You're excused," she said in a cold tone. She folded her arms so there was no chance for him to reach for her again. "It seems that it's a night of meeting old acquaintances. Martin meet my ex-boyfriend Trent."

Martin grinned and held out his hand. "Did that motorcycle ride terrify you too?"

Trent clenched his teeth and ignored the outstretched hand. She hadn't taken him on her motor-cycle yet. "She's trying to be funny."

Martin frowned. "I don't get the joke."

"Me neither," Trent said taking Erin's arm before saying in a low voice, "Either come with me or I will cause a scene that will get me arrested if I have to."

Erin took the hint and waved at Martin. "It was nice seeing you again."

He nodded. "Likewise."

Trent led her into a dark hall inside the club that was illuminated by blue neon lights along the trim. A large sign directing visitors to the restrooms hung at the end. They weren't alone, another couple was making out; another man paced mumbling something to himself, but at least it wasn't as crowded as the main room. Trent released her and said, "Okay, now listen—"

Erin pinned him with a hostile glare. "No, *you* listen.

I'm through pretending that you can't hurt me. That it's okay that you never compliment how I look or what I do for you. I'm tired pretending that it's okay that I'm always scheduling our time together." She hit her forehead. "And stupid me I was really excited about tonight because *you* made the suggestion. I even got a new dress. I thought tonight would be special. And at first it was nice, but then you changed and hardly looked at me once Xavier showed up. Did I not meet his standards or something?"

Trent shook his head. "I need you to listen—"

"I know *she* did," Erin continued. "The woman at the bar. He found her very intriguing. Obviously you did too."

"If you'll just listen—"

"To what? Your excuses? Just admit it and stop playing games with me. I know I'm not the most fascinating woman around but I don't like being treated like you're on the lookout for something better. I know. I get it. You were bored when I called you. We went out and had some fun, but you're a good looking, single guy who doesn't want to be exclusive for too long and..." She folded her arms. "Why do you keep rubbing your neck like that?" she demanded.

He shook his head. "It's nothing. Bad habit."

"I don't care. Why do you do it?"

"Sometimes my scar burns."

Her brows shot up. "It burns? You mean it hurts?"

He nodded.

"Does it also sting? Turn red?"

"I don't know."

She stepped closer. "The lighting here is terrible, but stay still and let me see." She removed his hand. "That's funny. It doesn't look—"

Trent pulled her roughly to him and held her tight. "I'm sorry," he whispered into her ear.

She stiffened, keeping her arms at her side. "You snake. You lied to me."

He nodded.

"You lie very well...I should be nervous."

He held her closer. "I'm not lying about this."

She tried to wiggle out of his grasp. "Let me go. I don't like being manipulated. You knew I was worried."

"I'm sorry, but I had to find a way to get you to listen to me and I need you to listen to me now." He drew back and searched her eyes. "I am sorry. She kissed me first and I let her. That was a mistake, but there was nothing more to it."

She pushed him away from her. "You liked it."

Not for the reason you think. He nodded. "I won't deny it. But that's all." He shook his head. "I don't know what my brother told you, but I'm—"

Erin stared at him, shocked. "That barracuda is your brother?"

Barracuda? "Yes and—"

"You two are related?"

"Yes, and—"

"By blood? He wasn't hatched from a—"

"Yes, by blood. We have the same father, though not the same mother. It's the same with my sister."

Erin lowered her head and spoke as if she were talking to herself. "No wonder there was such a strong resemblance." Her gaze met his. "Is he older or younger? Older, right?" She didn't give him a chance to reply. "He has to be that's why you were trying to impress him."

Trent blinked. "Uh..."

Erin nodded coming to a decision. "I think I get it now. That's why you changed when he came into the room. I'd wondered about that."

"Right, I messed things up. I did it wrong."

She narrowed her eyes. "You did *what* wrong?"

Everything! He softly swore. He couldn't tell her that he wouldn't have come to this club if his brother hadn't suggested it. He truly hated the acoustics and wished he'd taken her somewhere else. He couldn't tell her that he never met ex-girlfriends who kissed him and wanted him back or that he did notice her dress and thought she looked beautiful. "It's stupid."

"You didn't do it wrong. You tried to make me jealous and succeeded."

"Actually—"

"I have an older brother I try to impress too, but I don't hurt people trying to do it."

Trent hung his head. "I'm sorry." When he lifted his gaze he saw Erin staring at him in a strange way. "What?"

"I'm surprised you haven't gotten defensive yet."

"Defensive?"

"Yes." She lowered her voice in the imitation of a man. "How many times do you want me to say 'I'm sorry'? I told you I was. It meant nothing. Why won't you let it go?" She returned her voice to normal. "Like that."

Trent silently swore. She was right. She'd done a perfect imitation of his brother and how the new Trent was supposed to behave. He wasn't supposed to take the blame. He wasn't supposed to be understanding. He was supposed to make her feel needy and clingy. But he couldn't do that. *You're no match* for *her*, his brother had warned him. Would she see this as a weakness?

Erin clasped her hands together and bounced on the soles of her feet, a smile dancing around her lips. "Thank you." She sighed. "I was worried I was wrong about you. But I'm not."

Wrong about him? Wrong how? What was she talking about? What had he done right? He didn't care. He'd keep his mouth shut and go with the flow. She was happy now and that was all that mattered.

She rested her hands on her hips. "But you still deserve to be punished."

"I wouldn't go that far."

Erin turned on her heel.

Trent grabbed her wrist and spun her back to him. He'd lost control and needed to get it back again. "Okay, okay. I deserve it. I'll make this up to you. Let me take you to—"

Erin waved her finger. "No, I get to choose your punishment."

He swallowed, a sense of dread crawling over him. "Okay."

"And you won't like it but it's what you deserve."

Yes, he did. He was man enough to endure whatever she threw at him. "Fine, go ahead. I can take it," he said and an hour later he lived to regret those words.

CHAPTER 21

She wanted to sit on the couch, watch a funny movie and cuddle.

It was his kryptonite.

When Erin curled herself against his body Trent feared his eyes would roll to the back of his head in ecstasy. Yes, this was what he liked. It felt so good. He liked the sound of her steady breathing, the chime of Roger's collar as he shifted his head from his position on the floor. Trent loved to cuddle. He loved being touched. Dorothy used to tease him about it. It was nothing he'd admit to again. He liked the feel of a woman's soft curves against him. Not any woman, a woman he cared about. They'd both changed once arriving at his house.

He now wore jeans and a pressed short sleeved shirt (denying himself the orange T-shirt and grey sweatpants he usually liked to wear while relaxing) and Erin changed out of her gold dress into his blue, long sleeved shirt, tucking her bare legs underneath her.

Trent swallowed, as the curls of Erin's afro brushed against his chin, her breast pressed against his chest. So warm, sweet, soft, inviting.

She quickly sat up alarmed. "Am I hurting you?"

"What? No. Why?"

"You made a funny noise."

"It's nothing."

"This is probably torture for you, isn't it?" she said with a wicked laugh.

Yes, but not for the reason she suspected. He wished he could hold her closer. Stop pretending that he didn't care and relax and sink into her.

"No, it's fine."

"I know most guys don't like to cuddle. You—"

Having her looking up at him, while still being close didn't make it any easier. Her full, soft mouth was calling him even closer and if she didn't turn away soon he was going to kiss her. "I don't want to talk about it."

She narrowed her eyes. "Don't be mad at me. Remember that this is your fault."

He nudged her. "Watch the movie."

She studied him for a moment and part of him feared she'd say something, another part feared she'd pull away. But she didn't. She briefly (too briefly) kissed him on the lips then said, "Your punishment will soon end and I'll make it up to you later," before she settled back down beside him, snuggling with such intent he had to stifle another groan, and sighed content. "You are so comfortable."

He stiffened. That was a warning. Comfortable was dangerous. Comfortable was forgettable. Disposable.

Replaceable. Comfortable like a worn shoe, an old bed, a best friend. He could hear his brother chastising him. *You don't cuddle for no reason. You make her pay for it one way or another. Either it's foreplay, afterplay or play day is over.*

Trent briefly closed his eyes and gritted his teeth. No matter how good it felt, how much he liked it, how real it was...he had to break free. He suddenly smelled mint chocolate and opened his eyes and saw Erin holding up a cookie for him to eat. She still faced the TV. He sighed and took the cookie from her fingers being careful not to touch them, tempting as it was. She had a bag of the cookies on her lap. She'd picked it up at a convenience store before they'd arrived at his place.

"Do you like them?"

"Hmm." He was a sucker for anything sweet.

"I can get more."

"Hmm."

She fed him another cookie and to his relief they finished the movie in silence. He expected her to move away when the credits rolled but instead she turned to him. "That wasn't very funny, was it?"

"No, not really." He'd let her use his Guest account for his movie streaming service not wanting her to see what he usually liked to watch.

"We'll have to try something different next time."

"Sure."

Her gaze dropped to his throat.

He moved his shoulders feeling self-conscious. "What?"

"I've been thinking about your birthmark."

"What about it?"

She lightly touched it with her fingers. "It reminded me of something and I couldn't think of what it was until now."

He couldn't stop a grin, curious what she'd come up with. "What does it remind you of?"

"A trachea scar."

He froze.

She met his eyes. "Is it?"

"Why would I have a trachea scar?"

She sat up. "Possibly for the same reason you have a large scar down your neck."

"Maybe."

"What's the big secret?"

He shrugged, impatient. "No secret just not something I want to talk about."

Erin nodded. "Is that why you like that painting?" She pointed to the abstract his brother had gotten him. Trent hated it. He hated that none of the partially nude women were looking out. They all had their backs turned as if the artist were a voyeur looking in on them. He preferred more simple paintings with landscapes or bright colors.

"Hmm."

She looked around the room. "Where did you take the picture of Roger?"

"What?"

"The one where he was wearing headphones. I can't find it. I looked for it when I first came over to meet him, but couldn't figure out where you took it. Did you take the photo somewhere else?"

"Yes."

"Oh," she said, sounding a little disappointed. "That makes sense. The background looked a little messy and homey but your place is very orderly and cosmopolitan. I'm surprised you bought a house considering how much you like empty space. I would have thought you would have preferred something more...compact."

Trent felt his cheeks burn. How could she have seen so much in that picture he'd sent of Roger? "I like how sound moves through the house and I do experiments here."

"Oh." She nodded. "Yes, you must like the sound of rain hitting the rooftop, the tap of a breeze against the window. A house has a lot of sounds."

"Right."

She nodded to a silver statue on his bookshelf that reminded Trent of a phallic symbol. Xavier had assured him wasn't. "An amazing Ino piece, right? An example of true artistry."

"You like that?" he said surprised before he quickly corrected himself. "I mean...yes."

Erin crinkled her nose. "No, I don't particularly like it but I dated a guy who did. He was so passionate about art, especially Ino's but after a couple weeks I couldn't stand him." She covered her mouth. "Which has nothing to do with you. You're two very different people. Not all guys who like expensive wines, designer clothes and flashy cars are complete pricks."

"Right." Unfortunately, she was describing his brother to a T. But she was with him, right? Didn't that mean she liked it a little? If not on a subconscious level?

"Do you—?"

Trent kissed her because he didn't want her to notice anything else. Because he'd wanted to kiss her all evening. Because he didn't want to answer any more questions.

He kissed her because he hadn't lost her that night. Because her punishment had been sweet torture.

He kissed her slowly, aroused by how quickly her warm mouth surrendered to his. She tasted like no one else. Like a song he'd never heard before. She reminded him of his favorite sounds—the sound of a breeze rushing through a wheat field; fat raindrops against a tin roof; waves crashing along a beach, footsteps in the sand, crickets chirping in a still summer evening.

She made his redesigned home feel less empty, less of a facade. He didn't feel like he belonged there, but she did. She made it all worthwhile.

He deepened the kiss, thrilled when she did the same, taking the lead from him. Seizing his fiercely held control by touching the back of his neck, toying with the tight curls at the nape of his neck. No, no don't do that... not like that... That was his weakness. It was something he couldn't resist.

For the second time that night he felt his control slip away, but didn't care. He wanted more. Needed more. So much more.

CHAPTER 22

He had the looks of a devil and kissed like an angel. A naughty angel, but an angel all the same. Erin couldn't understand the contradiction. How could a man who owned a home like this—one which seemed designed for a man who didn't regard women very highly, not misogynistic but not with any true care, as if women were merely objects of pleasure—kiss like a man who loved women wholly and completely?

Trent kissed her like a man who was solid and true. Sexy and serious. Very, very serious. Like a man taking possession, making a vow, stating a claim. *You are mine.* It was like the kiss they'd had in the park. The kiss that made her stay despite her apprehensions.

Apprehensions. Every time she had them—the park, the club, his place—this man came through. This man who confused and delighted her. This man who made her believe that he truly wanted to be with her, only her. This was the man who'd held her in his arms and whispered an apology for what he'd done. Her heart had told her to reject him, to walk away. To save herself, but there had been a sincerity in his tone she'd never heard before. She believed him.

But was that her imagination again?

And this kiss. This wildly wondrous kiss that wrapped her in a velvet warmth. What did it mean?

Erin abruptly drew back and Trent looked hurt. He stared at her lips as if she'd taken a beloved toy away. "I should go," she said breathless.

Trent lifted his gaze to her face and she saw it—quick, brief, sudden—before it was gone. A vulnerable look. A look of such affection and dismay she was certain she'd imagined it.

"Hmm."

If you want me to stay, then tell me not to go, she silently pleaded, searching his eyes. *I won't go if you say so. Let me know how you feel.*

But he didn't. He bit his lip and looked away.

Erin stood feeling restless and irritated with herself. He'd kissed her, why did she have to make it a big deal? They'd had a good evening together. "I'd better go change."

"No."

"What?"

"I like you just the way you are." He pulled her down on his lap and kissed her again. She didn't resist. He wanted her to stay; she didn't need him to say the words. She wrapped her arms around his neck and her heart rejoiced.

This was the man she wanted to be with. Not the one

who had barely looked at her at the club, but the one who held her like this, tasted like this, kissed her like this.

This man who sometimes felt like a stranger. Who was he really? How could he kiss like this? Make her feel like this? And yet confuse her at the same time? What was going on in his mind? She never thought much of kissing before. With other men it was mildly interesting. But oh with him it was something new and wondrous. Exciting, thrilling, decadent.

She unbuttoned his shirt and kissed the scar at the hollow of his throat. Then kissed a little lower and stopped when she saw another scar. She briefly met his eyes. "Another bar fight?"

He nodded.

She trailed her finger down past his nipple and saw another faint scar. "The same?"

"Hmm."

She pressed her lips against it. "You really should stay out of bars."

"I'll remember that."

"However," she slowly traced the length of one scar before she lifted her gaze to meet his, "if you end up in my ER I'll take good care of you. Okay?"

He didn't reply but his eyes spoke volumes. She saw a bright, mischievous pleasure in his gaze that wiped away any remaining doubt and filled her with confidence. Her punishment didn't seem to have angered him at all. He seemed to be enjoying his time with her. She could be bold with him. She could be herself with him. She wouldn't scare him away.

She rubbed her hands together. "Let me see if I can

remember my ABCs. First I'd check your airway." She kissed him long and hard.

He pulled back. "Right now you're stopping my airway."

"Oh, sorry. Got carried away."

Trent slid his hand down the length of her bare leg, making her skin tingle. "What happens next?"

"Next?" Erin asked, losing her train of thought, caught up in the slow, sensuous rhythm of his hand traveling up and down her leg.

He nodded. "What comes after A?"

"B?"

Trent flashed a sexy grin. "Right, and what does B stand for, Doctor?"

Erin blinked. B? 'B' was a letter. What did B stand for? Oh, right she was discussing the ABCs. She crossed her legs, feeling her body grow damp, suddenly aware she was sitting on his lap. "Maybe I should stand for this."

He kept his arms around her and said in a low smooth voice, "What does B stand for?"

"Breathing." Something she was finding harder and harder to do.

"Am I breathing?"

She tilted her ear to his mouth. "Yes, you'll live."

He shook his head. "You forgot about C."

She didn't know where to go with C.

"Have you forgotten what it is?" he teased her.

"Circulation."

"And how is mine?"

She didn't dare move. Right now she knew blood was circulating through his body just find. She could feel the hard evidence of it in one key location and she was sitting on it.

"Don't get shy on me now," Trent said with laughter in his voice.

She cleared her throat and put on her professional voice. "I believe your circulation is fine and there's no constriction."

"I disagree."

"You do?"

"I think there's a lot of constriction."

Her eyes widened. "Is it because I'm sitting on it? Let me get up then."

Trent groaned. "No, that's not it and wiggling your butt like that doesn't make it any better."

Erin licked her lower lip. "Since the patient is very... responsive I think he can be discharged."

Trent shook his head. "I need to be admitted. I have an ache that won't go away."

She fanned her hand against his bare chest. "That sounds urgent."

"It is."

"You have to release me then."

"Why?"

"I have to find a spare bed."

Trent stood with her in his arms. "I already have one in mind."

CHAPTER 23

She knew how to touch him. Trent didn't know how or why but Erin's touch was like no other woman's. They lay naked in his master bedroom and he was as solid and erect as a flagpole, but Erin continued to take her time as she swept her hand over his body.

"I can't believe you're letting me do this," she said.

"What?"

"Let me touch you like this. I don't know why I enjoy it so much." She glanced at his erection. "I guess I've never had a man respond to me like this before."

"You're a virgin?"

"No," she said quickly looking suddenly shy. "I mean...no man's been so easy. So clearly interested."

He knew he was easy. An erection was easy for him because he liked to be touched. He especially liked to be touched by her. So she was right, the effect of her touch even shocked him. He'd never come so hard and fast before. And he wouldn't be able to stay still for long. If he didn't do something soon, he was going to come.

"Hold on a second." He reached over her and opened a drawer and pulled out a condom. "Want to do the honors?"

She shook her head.

Trent paused surprised. He thought she'd be eager. "Why not?"

Erin didn't meet his gaze. "I just think you should do it."

"I'll do it this time, but you'll do it next time. Okay?"

She made a noncommittal sound in her throat.

Trent rolled on the condom then said in a deep voice, "Now it's my turn to touch you."

Erin plastered on a smile as she inwardly cringed afraid she wouldn't like it. That the magic would be lost. She liked kissing and touching him but feared that the rest of it would be routine. *Relax. Don't tense up. Make sure he enjoys this.* She bit her lip, closed her eyes and waited. This was the part that men liked the most. He would be inside her and out within minutes. Maybe even seconds. Then it'd be over. She'd have to remember to groan. No, moan. Moaning would make him feel good. And he'd been patient with her it was his turn now. His turn to...why wasn't he doing anything?

Erin opened one eye and saw the ceiling. She'd expected to see Trent leaning over her. His scent lingered in the air, but had he gone somewhere? She opened both eyes and sat up. She turned and saw Trent lying on his side with his head in his hand, watching her.

"What are you doing?"

He drew her down beside him. "Let's try this again with your eyes open."

She shook her head, panic seizing her. "I can't." She held her breath and waited for the questions: Why not? What's wrong with you? Would it help if I put a bag over your head?

But Trent didn't say that. Instead he said, "Okay. Close your eyes and I'll tell you what I'm going to do. All right?"

"No."

"No?"

"You don't have to tell me." Why waste your time? It should take five minutes. Maybe ten.

"But I want to. I don't want you to have any surprises. Right now I'm going to touch your breasts."

Erin held her breath and waited for him to squeeze her like he would a ripe papaya. But instead of his hand she felt something wet and warm cover her nipple. Her eyes flew open. "You didn't say you were going to use your mouth."

"Oh," Trent said, feigning a look of surprise. "Did you want me to be more specific?"

"Yes, please," she added to soften her tone.

"Okay. I will. Close your eyes."

She did but this time she felt tense for an entirely different reason, not due to fear but anticipation.

"Now I'm going to touch your clit with the tip of my tongue. No, don't open your eyes."

"But you don't have to—"

"Don't you want me to have fun?"

"Yes."

"Good."

She felt the sheets move then felt him there, his tongue teasing her into ecstasy. He knew how to pleasure a woman. He was almost unnaturally attuned to her. He pleased her. He approached her body with careful attention, every touch was divine. Unhurried. As if he enjoyed every moment. His lovemaking matched his eyes. Kind, gentle, real.

But she knew it wasn't love. Not yet at least. Not for him. He didn't seem to know this about himself. How much he was revealing about his true nature and she wouldn't tell him. She was a lucky woman. She couldn't go back to a selfish, cloying man who made her feel as exciting as a corpse in bed. She couldn't get enough of this. Of him.

She felt herself grow moist and suddenly she didn't dread him inside her, she wanted him there. She opened her eyes. "Trent?"

"Yes."

"I'm ready for you."

He met her gaze and she saw a series of questions, but something in her eyes must have assured him because a satisfied smile touched his lips then he was inside. She welcomed him fully, keeping her eyes open to see the beautiful brown of his skin against the maroon bed sheets, hear the sound of his breathing and feel his hot flesh against hers. She didn't need to pretend to be somewhere else or to be someone else. She wanted to be present and fully alive to enjoy this moment and this man.

"You're not telling me what you're doing," she teased, tightening around him.

He clenched his teeth. "I can't."

Erin became alarmed. He sounded in pain. "Are you—"

He softly swore and said, "Don't move like that. I'm fine."

"But...you're enjoying this, right?"

Trent released a hollow laugh. "Are you for real?" He shook his head. "I can't believe you don't know what you do to me."

"As long as you like it."

"I like it." This time Trent was the one who had to close his eyes. He was falling hard and fast and knew it. He hadn't had sex with her the way the new Trent should. He should have kept his distance. He should have kept his walls up. He shouldn't have lost control and led with his heart, letting her know how much she meant to him. But for some reason when she touched him, he couldn't pretend to be someone else. He had to be completely himself. He could only hope she didn't notice. He never wanted her to know that every action was a silent plea that said "Stay with me" "Let me be your man."

He didn't open his eyes even when they finished. Even when Erin curled up against him in languid satisfaction and he drew her close to his body because it felt right.

He ignored the pounding of his heart, warning him of the danger he was in. He could never tell her how strong his feelings were for her. He'd made that mistake with the other women in his life. They didn't want his heart, they didn't need it so it wouldn't be something he offered her. Although he knew she was close to stealing it.

CHAPTER 24

Trent woke up to the sound of a thud. The room was still and dark, but he heard whimpering. "Quiet Roger," he said hoping his dog wouldn't wake Erin. Then he realized Erin wasn't in the bed beside him. He turned on the lights and saw her on the ground, grabbing her leg.

He scrambled out of bed and rushed to her. "What's wrong?"

Her face was contorted in pain; she couldn't speak but could only point to her leg.

He could immediately guess the reason seeing her leg stretched out in a spasm.

"It's okay, baby. Hold on," he said rubbing the hard muscle. Slowly it began to ease and she started to sit up then her thigh tightened and she was on the ground again, biting her lip. The second cramp took longer to settle and he swore hating to see her suffer. Finally, the muscle relaxed and he heard her sigh. "Thanks," she said in a hoarse whisper.

"Let me help you back into bed."

"I'm afraid to move."

"We'll take it slowly." He helped her into a sitting position. She sank against him, her back to his chest. "Can't we just stay like this for a minute?"

"Okay." Trent pulled the blanket from off the bed and wrapped it around them.

"I'm sorry I woke you. I felt the cramp coming on and I thought I could stop it."

"Don't apologize." He began to drape the blanket higher around her shoulders then stopped when he saw a bruise high up on her upper arm. Why hadn't he noticed before? "Does this hurt?" he asked lightly touching it.

"Not anymore." She laughed. "And it wasn't my fault. A confused older gentleman came into the ER, which is not uncommon, and as I was checking his pulse he grabbed me and wouldn't let go. He kept calling me by another woman's name." She paused. "I think it was Maureen. Anyway, he wouldn't let go. We finally had to subdue him, but what a grip. It's been a crazy week."

"Have you made the drinks I told you about?"

"I will," Erin said in the small voice of a child afraid to get into trouble.

Trent sighed in frustration. "You can't push yourself like this and not expect—"

"I know. I'm sorry. Truly." She sounded sleepy.

He held her close. He wanted to take care of her. Protect her. But that was the old Trent. He was the new

Trent now. He had to remember that. "Come on," he urged her. "You can't fall asleep here."

"Oh yes I could. You smell so good and are so comfortable."

Trent gritted his teeth. There was that damn word again—comfortable. He didn't want her to think of him like that. He removed the blanket, surprised by how cool the room felt against his bare skin without it. He lifted her to her feet and she hobbled back to bed. The old Trent would have carried her; the new Trent kept his hands at his side. He replaced the blanket on the bed then got under the covers. This time when Erin snuggled against him, he didn't pull her closer.

CHAPTER 25

Trent didn't like to plead or beg, but he was desperate. He stood outside Mindy's apartment door with a small cooler containing two replenishment drinks he'd mixed. He met her frown with a smile determined to get his way. He knew she'd just come home from work and wasn't in the mood for visitors, but he needed her to do him a favor.

"Why would I do that?" Mindy said after he told her his request.

Trent held the containers out and widened his smile. "Because I asked you nicely."

Mindy rested against the doorframe and folded her arms unmoved. "Why can't you drop them off at the hospital yourself?"

"It looks better coming from you."

"No, it doesn't."

"Mindy please. You pass the hospital on your way to work."

"I don't care. It's a lie. I didn't make these drinks for her. You did."

And Erin couldn't know that. "Just this once." He pushed past her and set the cooler in her kitchen.

Mindy closed the door with extra force. "No."

"This is not for me. This is for her. She needs these drinks. You should have seen the pain she was in the other night."

Mindy's expression softened. "Pain?"

"Yes, agony," Trent said pleased to see his cousin weaken. "It was bad and it's all because she works hard and gets dehydrated but doesn't notice." He tapped the cooler. "These drinks can prevent that." He shoved his hands in the pockets of his jeans. "I won't ask you to do it again."

Mindy sat at the kitchen table and grumbled, "You know I don't like you making me part of your scheme."

"Think of it as a 'thanks' for giving Sunny a good home."

She narrowed her eyes. "You're sneaky."

He grinned and pushed the cooler towards her. "I know."

"How long have you been seeing her now? Five months?"

"Nearly four."

She held her head and groaned. "I never knew how much I'd regret making that stupid bet with you."

"Forget the bet." He kissed her affectionately on the cheek. "Think of this as supporting a good cause."

She lifted her head and glared at him. "I'll never see it that way, but I don't like the idea of Erin in pain. Fine," she said with reluctance. "I'll do it. But that had better be it."

BRANDON STARED AT HIS SISTER AMUSED AS SHE AND Tara sat on the couch together going over Tara's latest crime story. Erin had provided her with the details of a survivable gunshot wound. But after that Erin could talk of nothing else but the surprise she'd received at the hospital.

"And they taste so delicious," Erin said. "I couldn't believe Mindy took the time to give them too me. She told me that Trent had mentioned to her about my muscle cramps and she wanted to help. She's got a big heart. She even typed up little instructions to let me know that they'd only last three days and how to make my own."

"You're making me want to try some," Brandon said.

"You should." Erin stopped as an idea came to her. "You should both meet them. Brandon, you've already met her, but Tara you should too. I'd like to have a casual get together." She sent her brother a pleading look. "But I'd need some help."

Seeing his sister so happy made him soften. He was ready to meet the guy she'd been talking about. "When and where?"

"At my place, I'll figure out when."

But when Erin told Trent of her plan he was less than enthused.

"Why would you want to do that?" he asked on a late night walk with Roger, autumn leaves scattering along the pavement. Roger trotted beside them with his tail happily wagging. In his mouth he held his latest treasure —a small black glove with pink stars.

"Why not? She went out of her way and I want to thank her."

"You could have sent a text."

"This is better."

"They're just drinks," he grumbled.

"They're not just drinks," Erin said offended. "They're more than that. You could have told her about my leg cramps and she could have ignored or dismissed you, but she didn't. She took the time to buy the ingredients, follow the recipes and deliver them to me. Your cousin is amazing."

"Should I start calling her Saint Mindy?"

"I wouldn't go that far. But you can start by calling her and inviting her to my place for dinner."

CHAPTER 26

She served spicy-sweet glazed shrimp over a bed of yellow rice and a pineapple tart for dessert.

"This is amazing," Mindy said as they all sat around Erin's tiny dining table.

"Don't thank me," Erin said. "Thank Brandon. I only made the dessert he did the rest."

Trent stared at the other man shocked. "You cooked this?"

Brandon sent him a hooded look. "Is that a problem?"

"No," he said quickly, feeling heat steal up his neck. His tone had been all wrong. He could understand Brandon being defensive. He'd been the same way in the past. The old Trent would have asked him where he'd gotten the shrimp and how he'd managed the light coconut flavor in the rice, but the new Trent stayed silent.

Tara smiled at her husband with pride. "Brandon's a wonderful cook. All I have to do is wash the dishes."

Trent stared at the couple in both awe and confusion.

Brandon looked like an average guy like him or rather like he used to be. "How did you two meet?"

"We were high school sweethearts," Brandon said, watching him. "Which probably sounds soppy to you."

No, it sounded incredible.

Tara rested her head on Brandon's shoulder. "In my sophomore year I broke my ankle while on a family vacation and was so upset because I'd wanted to try out for the track team that year. Brandon helped keep my spirits up and carried my books between classes even if that sometimes made him late for his own. He was already my best friend but that day he became something more." She lifted her head and smiled at him. "I've loved him ever since."

Her best friend? She loved him? They'd been together since high school?

Trent cleared his throat hoping his tone didn't sound judgmental. "Wasn't college difficult?"

Tara frowned. "Why would it be difficult?"

"There are so many other people to meet," he said, echoing the words of one girl who refused to give him a chance for that very reason. I'm not ready to get serious, she'd said.

Tara shrugged. "Sure there were lots of other guys, but I was as committed to Brandon as he was to me and that was fine for us."

"I know what you're thinking," Brandon said, his gaze level and ready for combat. "You can't believe I've only been with one woman."

"I didn't say anything," Trent said, sensing the tension in the air.

"You didn't have to."

"Don't put words in his mouth," Erin said with a nervous laugh. "He was only curious about you two."

"Doesn't matter. Most people think we missed out on something, but they don't understand. Most people see life like a banquet and they are hungry. Constantly hungry for more. People like Tara and me..." He paused as if collecting his thoughts. "The moment we met we were full and were weren't hungry for anything else. We were lucky. It doesn't always happen that quickly, but it does happen. When you're with the right one, you don't need anything or anyone else."

"Right," Trent said not knowing what else to say. He was stunned. Brandon was a wonder to him. How had he managed it? How had he escaped staying in the friend-zone? How had he managed to get someone to love him and marry him without playing games?

Trent avoided Mindy's gaze, although he felt it. He didn't believe this. It was a trick of the eye. Tara was an exception. Brandon had gotten lucky, he'd admitted it. Their relationship wasn't the norm. Trent knew it. He'd proven it. Most women weren't like her. They didn't fall in love with their best guy friends; they relegated him to the friend-zone and left him there.

Erin would have been bored with the old Trent by now, if she'd even have given him a chance at all. She'd mentioned being attracted to guys like his brother, and he still remembered his brother's sly grin when he said that she was just his type.

His type—Xavier's not Trent's. She'd dated a guy like Xavier before and knew about the artist Ino. Somebody he'd never heard of before now. He'd seen the guy she'd brought to Dorothy's wedding. She wasn't the type to like safe and dependable. She rode a motorcycle and liked the noise and chaos of the ER. She needed excitement. She sought that in her personal life and he'd give it to her. He'd keep their relationship interesting.

Sure she sometimes complained about having to plan most of their time together and not getting enough compliments, but didn't she stay? Sometimes women complained but they didn't really mean it. If he changed, she'd break up with him as all the others had.

"If you haven't guessed," Erin said breaking the silence, "my brother is a romantic."

"Which is sweet," Mindy said, stressing the word. "Something that's not bad for a guy to be."

"It's not something you want to admit to either," Trent said.

"The only opinion that matters to me is Tara's," Brandon said. "The rest can go to—"

"I think we should change the subject," Erin said.

Trent shook his head. "Like you said, you got lucky. You don't have to worry about things like that."

Brandon's gaze darkened. "You think women only prefer guys like you?"

Erin jumped to her feet and said in a bright voice, "Let's play a game of charades."

"Not all but most," Trent replied. "I have a record to prove it while you don't."

Brandon winced and Trent knew he'd hit his mark, but the other man quickly recovered.

"I feel sorry for guys like you," he said. "You think

you have women all figured out, but the truth is you're at the buffet eating everything in sight and you're still starving. One day you'll find yourself still hungry and alone."

For a brief moment Trent thought of his father. Three ex-wives, numerous girlfriends and three children, but he'd spent his last birthday alone because none of them wanted to be with him.

Brandon glanced at his sister with a mix of love and regret. "I don't even think you know what you have."

"You don't know me at all," Trent said.

Brandon returned his gaze to him. "I know you better than you think."

Erin walked over to her brother and pulled his arm. "Come and help me with the dishes. Everyone go rest in the living room."

Brandon nodded, but by the look in his eyes, Trent knew he'd made an enemy.

CHAPTER 27

"What came over you?" Erin said once she was alone with Brandon in the kitchen. She set some dishes in the sink and they settled with a clatter.

Brandon set a dish on the counter. "I don't like him."

"You got off on the wrong foot." She turned to him and rested against the sink. "Give him some time to grow on you." She pointed at him when he opened his mouth. "And don't say 'like mold'."

He opened his mouth wider.

She wagged her finger. "Or like fungus. Or bacteria. Or anything else disgusting."

He closed his mouth and shook his head. "I still don't like him."

He hadn't liked any of the men in Erin's life, but for some reason Trent bothered him the most. And he couldn't figure out why. It wasn't just the clothes or the attitude, but something else. Brandon inwardly sighed.

He also couldn't ignore that Trent had hit a sore spot. He'd been fighting guys like him all his life. People who treated him as if he were a freak or a relic from another century. As if his love for his wife was somehow quaint and cute. As if it made him weak in return. But he knew love made a man strong. Especially the real, deep constant love of someone who'd pledged their life to you.

Sure he wasn't complex like other guys. There was no mystery to him. He loved his wife, his sister, his parents, and his job. How boring could that be? But he'd created the life he wanted for himself. And he grew tired of feeling that he had to defend his choice.

No, he hadn't looked at another woman. No, he wasn't secretly gay. Yes, he could imagine growing old with her. Fifty years didn't feel long at all.

He wanted the same for his sister. A good man, an honest man. A man who could take her strange quirks and love her all the same. Brandon knew Trent wasn't that guy, but he also knew Trent made her happy and he didn't want to spoil that. In time, she'd see what who he was and break up with him. But he didn't look forward to the next man she'd choose.

He blinked when he felt water on his face.

"Earth to Brandon," Erin said, wiping her hands on a dish towel after splashing him with her wet hand.

"Sorry."

"At least he's better than Jeremiah."

"A mummified corpse would be an improvement over him." But Jeremiah had been harmless. Vain, selfish, but easy to read and easy to spot.

Trent was something different entirely. He wasn't as

showy as the rest. He had an air of mystery that set Brandon on edge and Trent's relationship with Erin had lasted longer than the others. Brandon sighed and wondered he'd if he'd encouraged his sister to get away from a shark and run straight into the arms of a wolf.

BRANDON DIDN'T LIKE HIM.

Trent wasn't used to that. People usually did. He was the kind of guy who got along with most people. It served him well in business, people liked to work with him and in his personal life he usually easily won over parents, aunts and uncles and grandparents.

Unfortunately, he didn't want to marry them. The new Trent wasn't supposed to care. All that mattered was what Erin thought.

But that didn't stop him from feeling the cold gaze of her brother on him.

Trent felt the other man's gaze on him throughout the evening as they played charades. It didn't help that Mindy kept watching him too. He'd actually had to pay her to come.

"You said only one favor," she'd said when he'd called her.

"She only wants to thank you."

"I don't like being part of your lie."

"Five hundred."

"What?"

"I'll give you half of what you paid me for the bet. How's that?"

"Fine, but make it cash."

At least he'd gotten his money's worth. Mindy was her same bubbly self and didn't give him away, but the way her gaze drifted from Brandon and Tara to him and Erin spoke volumes. It was as if she was saying "See what you could have had if you'd just been yourself?" But he knew her observation was skewed. Tara and Erin were nothing alike. But the comparison bothered him. He had to be on guard, which was why he and Erin had lost the game of charades. He couldn't focus.

Mindy made a comment about Sunny and Tara offered to show her how the cat was getting on and the three women left the apartment to go to Brandon and Tara's place, but not before Erin kissed Trent on the cheek and whispered something in Brandon's ear.

The moment the door closed, Brandon said, "Two more weeks."

"What?"

"That's how long I give you."

"Listen, I—"

Brandon shook his head. "You don't have to explain. I've seen the pattern especially with guys like you. But you bothered me more than most and I couldn't figure out why until now. You're not like the rest. You're a fraud."

Trent shrugged his Xavier shrug. *Show no fear. Act like it doesn't matter.*

"You know why I know you're a fraud?" Brandon continued. "Because I now remember seeing you at Derrick's wedding, but I also remember seeing you some-where else. So I'll ask you this. Are you still in love with another woman?"

Trent froze. No one was supposed to know that. He forced a laugh. "I don't know what you're talking about."

Brandon rubbed his hands together, a malicious grin tugging on the corner of his mouth as if he were enjoying Trent's discomfort. "Let me refresh your memory. I was able to make it to a party my cousin Derrick had with his new girlfriend now wife. I remember seeing you there. Erin couldn't make it because of her schedule. If she had gone, she'd probably remember you too."

Trent shrugged again, his heart picking up speed. The old Trent wasn't memorable. How could Brandon remember him from a crowded event more than a year ago? "So what? I'm a memorable guy."

Brandon shook his head. "I don't remember you for the reasons you think, but the look on your face. Especially the way you looked at Dorothy."

Trent swallowed, his throat feeling as dry as the Sahara.

"Somehow...I don't know how, but my extended family is big and likes to talk, I found out that you were her ex but you'd remained friends." He rubbed his chin. "I think I once heard her describe you as her 'sweet, adorable pet'."

Trent's tone hardened. "She was talking about someone else. Unlike you I was not the only man in Dorothy's life."

"True. But it was the expression on your face that day I won't forget because I saw it again on her wedding day."

Trent took a deep breath, hearing his brother's voice. *Don't explain. Don't argue. Don't pick up a hot ball unless you want to get burned.*

Brandon narrowed his gaze at Trent's silence then nodded as if coming to a conclusion. "I see. That's how you're going to play it. Fine. I'm going to pretend that it's all just coincidence. That of all the women you could have met at the wedding you decided to date the cousin of your ex-girlfriend's new husband."

"It's a small world."

Brandon's cruel grin returned. "Exactly. Which means I'll be watching you. So you'd better decide whether you want to keep dating—no using—my sister as revenge against your ex to show her what she's missing or if you'll move on."

Damn. Damn. Damn. He was caught. Mindy had always warned him about his face. Why had he worn his heart on his sleeve so long ago? Why hadn't he chosen someone who wasn't related to Derrick? Then they wouldn't have known anything about his past. Trent frantically searched his mind. He had to regain the upper hand. If not, he'd lose. He couldn't afford to lose. It wasn't his pride that was at stake, it was Erin.

The old Trent would have explained and apologized and he felt words to that effect on the tip of his tongue, but he stopped. He wasn't that man anymore and he didn't have to explain. He could love whomever he wanted and date whomever he wanted. He wouldn't let anyone tell him what to do. He couldn't get on the defensive. Xavier wouldn't. He'd fight.

"If you don't want your sister to get hurt I suggest you stop trying to warn me off," Trent said in a soft, mocking tone. "Or else I will make sure to make her fall for me even more than she already has. And if you think in any way you can dissuade her from doing so I'd like to see you try."

Brandon's eyes narrowed. "So it's a game."

"No, I don't like people telling me what toys I get to play with. I tend to get a little possessive."

"So do I."

"We both know the more you tell her to stay away from me the more curious she'll become." Trent shrugged. "It's your choice. Let things fall as they may or interfere and make my job easier."

The sound of a key in the lock, stopped Brandon's reply, but his dark, brown eyes said, "We'll see."

Trent watched Brandon smile at Tara and Erin and listen to them talk about how Mindy played with Sunny.

He understood the other man's dislike. He imagined himself in Brandon's shoes. If someone was messing with his sister he'd do the same thing. He'd do his best to protect her and he had exposed him as a fraud. He was. He'd initially toyed with Erin in order to win a bet and had succeeded, but now he'd gotten caught.

Now he was in too deep. Even if Erin learned he was Dorothy's ex-boyfriend and heard stories about him, he'd lie his way out of them. He'd gotten good at lying and wearing a mask and he'd do it to keep her by his side. She was too precious to him. And the new Trent wasn't backing down.

CHAPTER 28

"She's like a ramped up robot," Mindy said in a low voice as she and Trent both sat in the living room and watched Erin clean up in the kitchen. Brandon and Tara had gone home after Erin had kindly shooed them away, thanking them for all that they'd done, but letting them know she could manage cleaning up by herself. "I can't believe she got off a major shift at the hospital and managed to entertain us like this, even with the help of her brother. The food was delicious and now she's cleaning everything up." She pointed to herself. "Now, if it were me, first there would only be paper plates and—"

Trent didn't hear the rest. When he looked at Erin she didn't look like a robot in high gear, she looked like a woman who was exhausted and on the verge of collapse. "You should go home," he interrupted, leaving Mindy open mouthed in mid-sentence.

"What about you?"

I am home, he almost said before he stopped himself. "What about me?"

"Are you going to leave Roger alone all night?"

"Roger is fine."

Mindy paused then said, "Did you hear what her brother said?"

Every word and they still echoed in his thoughts. Trent stood. "It's not polite to overstay your welcome."

"I'm just saying you might have a chance if—"

"I'm not taking advice from a man who's..." *Never had his heart broken*, he silently finished.

Mindy folded her arms, her voice hard. "Who's what?"

"Go home."

She sent him a long look. "I really like her. I was hoping I wouldn't." She pinched his leg.

"Ow!" He rubbed his thigh. "What was that for?"

"Because you've made a mess of everything."

He lifted her out of her seat. "Everything is fine. Now go home."

She raised her voice. "Bye Erin, thanks for everything."

"Would you like some leftovers?" Erin asked her.

Mindy's face lit up. "Oh that would be—"

"Unnecessary," Trent cut it as he shoved her towards the door. "Bye Mindy."

She shot him a nasty look then left.

Trent sighed, feeling the tension within him ease. Just him and Erin, alone at last. He walked up behind Erin as she dipped a large serving plate into the soapy water. For some reason she smelled like sugar and lemons then he noticed the dish detergent she was using was Lemony Burst. He slid his hand down her arm, liking the warm feel of her skin beneath his fingers, before he covered her hand and whispered, "It was a great evening."

She started to scrub the plate. "Thanks."

"Why didn't you stack the dishwasher?"

She paused then shrugged. "I needed something to do."

"You hadn't thought of using it, had you?"

"Not until now," she admitted with a laugh.

"Well, now I'll be your dishwasher." He took the sponge from her then nuzzled her neck. "You already know how to turn me on."

"I wouldn't want you to get overheated. I had that happen once and—"

"I won't overheat. Don't worry and relax." He felt her lean against him and sensed the weight of her exhaustion. "You could have ordered in."

"I told you, Brandon cooked."

"And you did the dessert." He kissed her cheek, which was a mistake because then he wanted to kiss her mouth. He took a deep breath and tried to focus on washing the dishes. "I liked that part of the meal the best."

"Did Mindy like it?"

Trent sighed hearing the worry in her voice and rested his chin on her shoulder. "Yes, of course."

"Good." She hesitated.

"What is it? You're still tense."

"Sorry about my brother."

"Don't be. He cares about you."

"A little too much, maybe."

No, he knows what you deserve, Trent wanted to say, but hesitated and quietly continued helping Erin wash up until there were only two dishes left. "I'll finish these. Go sit down."

"Are you sure?"

He winked at her. "This dishwasher was built to last."

With no further protest Erin left the kitchen, went into the living room and turned on the TV. Trent packaged all of the leftovers in various containers and put them away, then straightened the pots. When he returned to the living room he found Erin fast asleep on the couch, the TV still on full blast. He lifted the remote to turn it off then stopped. She'd once told him she liked to fall asleep to noise so he'd keep it on a little while longer.

He covered her up with a blanket before he looked around the room. Erin had moved some furniture for their game of charades; Mindy had left crumbs from where she'd indulged in an extra tart and left a ring stain on a side table from her glass so he put things back in place and cleaned up the best he could.

Once he was done, Trent looked at Erin sleeping and saw a slight smile on her face. He grinned at the sight. She reminded him of a happy, tired puppy. He was glad she'd liked the replenishment drinks, now if only he could find a way to make sure she didn't burn herself out. If she wasn't careful that was a real possibility.

He knelt in front of her and studied her peaceful, sleeping face.

"I'm going to look after you. You won't know it, but I will." He drew the covers up higher and smiled at her happy, soft sigh. He started to stand but paused when he heard a sound.

The sound of an intruder breaking the intimate peace between him and Erin.

Trent turned swiftly and saw Brandon standing in the doorway, a surprised expression on his face. Trent rushed over to him shock and anger making his heart pound. How long had he been there? What had he seen? He quickly closed the distance between them, then said in a low voice, "What are you doing here?"

"I-I came to check on Erin. I have a spare key." He held it up. "I didn't expect..." His words trailed off.

"You didn't expect me to still be here," Trent finished.

Brandon nodded.

"As you can see she's fine."

Brandon looked past Trent to his sister sleeping on the couch then back at Trent. He softly swore. "Does she know?"

Trent rubbed his thumb and forefinger together anxious to pretend that he hadn't been caught with his guard down. He wanted to control the situation and see Brandon leave. He'd had enough of him today. "Know what?"

"How you really feel?"

Trent winced and silently swore. Did he go on the defensive? Laugh and deny it? To be exposed twice in one night was just sloppy. He should have gone home like Mindy said, but it was too late now. He folded his arms and narrowed his eyes. "Don't pretend to know me or read too much into what you saw."

The corner of Brandon's mouth kicked up in a grin. "At least I can hate you a little less now."

"No, I think your first instincts were right."

Brandon held his gaze. "I think that's what you want me to believe."

Trent didn't flinch. "I don't care what you think."

Brandon nodded. "And I believe you." He shrugged. "I don't know what you're up to, but I'm curious to see where it leads."

"Hmm."

Brandon opened the front door. "I'll be watching."

"You can watch from a distance," Trent said.

"Distance?"

"You won't need to check on her anymore."

Brandon couldn't stop a smile. "Because she's got you?"

"Exactly."

"That's fine, but you're going to have to get your own key."

"Don't worry. I plan to."

CHAPTER 29

Brandon returned home in a daze. He still couldn't believe what he'd seen. It was...incredible.

Against Tara's advice he'd gone to Erin's place determined to tell her what Trent was all about. He didn't want to give the bastard two weeks, he wanted him gone. And he didn't care if Erin didn't believe him at first; he planned to wear her down until she saw what he did.

He knew a guy like Trent wouldn't hang around long so he waited for what he thought was a decent amount of time before he went back to her place. He knocked, but nobody answered, so he used his key, imaging her asleep on the couch were she usually crashed after a long day with the TV left on or the sound of international hip-hop artists blaring from her speakers.

And that's where he found her.

But she wasn't alone.

He was there.

Trent was still there. And he was taking care of her. Brandon couldn't believe his eyes. The place was clean. He watched Trent rest a broom against a chair then pull Erin's covers up a little more. But it wasn't that action that shocked him; it was the other's man expression.

It wasn't the same as when he'd looked at Dorothy, but it was close. Trent was not what he seemed. He hid it well. So damn well that Brandon had completely missed it, but at that moment Brandon had seen the truth. He saw that look: The look of devotion. Trent really cared about Erin. He was in it for the long haul. That's when Brandon knew he wouldn't interfere. He wanted this for his sister. He wasn't sure it would last, but he hoped it would. He was so shocked he'd dropped the keys and caught Trent's attention. And the expression on Trent's face was one of rage. For a brief moment he was afraid. He felt like he'd stepped into the territory of a grizzly bear. Trent's eyes flashed with the promise of violence. He would protect what was his.

"Well?" Tara asked him when Brandon came through the front door. She held Sunny in her arms and was stroking the kitten's head. "Is she okay?"

Brandon hesitated. He hadn't told her the real reason he'd gone to see his sister—all his suspicions or his conversation with Trent—but he had shared that he was worried about her and wanted to check to make sure she was okay. "She's fine."

"I guess you worried for no reason."

Brandon set his sister's key on the side table and nodded. "I think you're right."

SHE HADN'T MEANT TO FALL ASLEEP, BUT SHE WAS grateful for the reprieve.

Had she really felt Trent's strong chest against her back, his arms on either side of her as she washed the dishes? They had felt arousing and comforting at the same time. She remembered talking about a dishwasher... and did he mention her dessert or something? It was all fuzzy now but had felt so good. It must have been a dream. She couldn't imagine Trent spending time with her in the kitchen doing that.

Erin opened her eyes and felt the weight of a blanket covering her. It reached right up to her nose. She heard the murmur of voices from the TV. She pulled the blanket down and glanced up to see Trent's arm along the back of the couch.

She sat up alarmed. "How long have I been out?"

He kept his gaze on the screen. "Not long. Relax, you haven't missed your shift or anything."

She sighed, relieved, although a little embarrassed that she was so easy to read. Of course she hadn't slept for days although it felt like it. Before she could ask him the exact length of her nap, he said, "How do you feel?"

Something in his voice made her sense something was wrong. That's when she also realized something else...her couch felt very warm and smelled incredibly good. She turned from the TV and glanced up and saw the bottom of Trent's chin.

His chin? Why was she looking at his chin?

She swallowed as a slow dawning came over her: She

was on his lap. She quickly scrambled off. "I am so sorry. I can't believe I did that."

"It was quite a feat," Trent said impressed. "I sat down beside you and the next thing I knew you stretched your legs out across my lap."

"Why didn't you push them away?"

He ignored her. "Then you wiggled your way down until you were halfway on my lap. You wrapped your arms around my waist and you were fine for a while then shimmied your way up my chest and stayed like that until you woke up."

"I am so sorry."

"I didn't say I didn't enjoy it."

"It's still embarrassing." She wrapped the blanket tight around her. "I don't know why I find you so comfortable."

She didn't know what she said wrong, but he suddenly frowned and turned off the TV. "I should go."

"Just a couple more minutes." She patted her lap. "You can take a nap now."

"I'm not tired."

"You can pretend to be. Or," she opened the blanket, "you can join me."

He hesitated.

"It's not officially cuddling. It's just sharing a blanket. I know you don't like to cuddle."

Trent bit his lip and sighed. "Actually, the truth is—"

"Wait," Erin suddenly said looking around the room in amazement. "Did you clean up?"

"Umm—"

She slapped her forehead. "Of course you didn't.

Was it Mindy? I bet it was. I was so tired I didn't notice before she left."

Erin sensed him pause before he said, "Right, Mindy hates a mess. She likes to tidy things up. Yes, she did all this before she left."

"I'll have to thank her."

"No," he said quickly. "She's shy with praise," he added when Erin gave him a strange look. "You've already done more than enough. Anything more and you'll make her feel uncomfortable."

Yes, her brother had warned her that she could be overwhelming. "Okay, but make sure you tell her. The place looks amazing."

Trent bit his lip then shook his head. "I can't do this anymore. There's something I need to tell you."

She didn't want to hear it. She sensed something was wrong but didn't want to face it. Everything had seemed perfect until this moment but something had changed. She'd said something wrong. Did something wrong. But what? What could have made him look like that? When had she made a mistake? What had gone wrong? The evening had been lots of fun except for... Erin sighed as a thought came to her.

"Erin, the truth is—"

She rushed to her feet eager to stop him. "I already have a brother."

Trent blinked. "What?"

She took his hand. "I know what Brandon said tonight bothered you, but I don't want you to worry. He has a different type of guy in mind that he wants for me. Someone more like him, but I don't need that. I already have a brother, a great one, so I don't need another one. I don't need you to worry about me or look after me." She laughed. "I don't know what I'd do with a guy like Brandon. I love him of course, but...he's too much of an open book. I like a little mystery. I like you just the way you are."

Trent stared at her and died a little at that moment.

He listened to Erin's words and her laughter and felt his heart split in two. There was no going back now. *I like you just the way you are.* There was no chance for the old Trent to emerge. She wouldn't want him.

"Okay?" Erin said in an eager voice, searching his eyes.

He nodded unable to speak. He couldn't make a sound. He felt as if his vocal muscle had been seized.

She sat back down on the couch and patted the space beside her. "Just five more minutes then you can go."

He kissed her on the cheek. "No, I have to go now," he said in a soft voice before he left.

CHAPTER 30

"So when do I get to meet her?" Vince asked Trent as they sat in the control room of the studio after helping one of his clients with her recording.

"Who?"

"Your theory. It's been months."

"I know."

"Well?"

"You won't meet her."

"It's over?"

"Hmm."

Vince knew better than to push. Trent could get into his silent moods either when a project at work wasn't going well or a relationship. He wondered if this "theory" had forced his friend to change how he dressed or had made him act less open and friendly than he used to be. There was a cool, distant air about him now that Vince didn't like, but accepted. He decided to change the subject.

He looked at the images on the screens in his digital workstation. "You should hear Aunt Sally go on about this doctor who helped Cathy. They go on and on about her like she's Wonder Woman. If you didn't hate doctors so much—"

"I'm seeing her."

Vince stopped with his hands halfway over the keyboard. "What?"

"I'm seeing a doctor."

Vince spun around to him and swore. "Is it serious?"

Trent nodded, grim. "Very."

"Terminal?"

Trent frowned. "What are you talking about?"

"Your diagnosis. Is it terminal?"

"Who said anything about a diagnosis?"

"You said you're seeing a doctor."

Trent sighed. "I meant, I'm dating one."

"No, you're not."

"Yes, I am."

"You don't date doctors."

"I do now."

Vince sat back in his chair and stared at Trent's dark trousers and grey shirt. He used to wear jeans or khakis and a sweater when it got cold. Now he looked like a man always ready for the club. "Is she the reason you're dressing like that?"

Trent lifted a brow and said in a low voice, "Something wrong with my clothes?"

He was itching for a fight and Vince didn't know

why. Something was wrong with his friend and it worried him. "Is this because of Dorothy?" Vince asked in a cautious voice.

"What's wrong with my clothes?"

"It's not you."

Trent sighed annoyed. "Why does everyone keep saying that?"

"Because it's true. Listen, if this woman is trying to change you—"

"I didn't say that."

"Who is she?"

Trent stood and patted him on the back. "You didn't need me for this session either."

He didn't, but lately Trent had been a hard man to get a hold of and now he understood why. This woman was trying to make him into another man. He didn't laugh and smile as easily as he used to. His advice and suggestions weren't as generous and deeply thought out as they'd been in the past. He feared he'd lose his friend for good to some unknown woman he hadn't met yet. "Wait..." Vince suddenly said as Trent grabbed the door handle, a thought coming to him. "When I mentioned Cathy's doctor you said 'I'm seeing her'."

Trent nodded.

Vince's brows shot up. "You're seeing the doctor who helped Cathy?"

He nodded again.

"Why?"

He rested against the door and folded his arms. "I told you I was working on a theory."

Vince noticed the defensive pose and knew to tread

carefully. Dorothy had been bad for him but this woman was ten times worse. "And did you come up with anything?"

"Yes."

Vince waited. "Care to tell me about it?"

"No."

"Will I get to meet her?"

"Probably not."

Vince started to grin. "Then again, I don't need your permission." *Especially since I now know her name and where she works.*

Trent narrowed his eyes. "Stay away from her."

It was a warning he didn't plan to obey. His friend was in danger and he was going to make sure he got him out of it. This woman may be a great doctor but she was a lousy girlfriend if she was making him change like this.

He had to meet the enemy.

CHAPTER 31

"What else did you say to him?" Erin demanded later the following day after her shift. She sat in her brother's living room while he played with Sunny on the floor swaying a string with a fuzzy yellow bobble on the end back and forth, the scent of their spicy chicken dinner still in the air.

"What?" Brandon said.

"Trent almost dumped me the other night."

"What?"

"Stop saying that."

"I don't know what you're talking about." He watched Sunny quickly lose interest in the string and jump up next to Erin who began to stroke her. "Sunny seems to miss you when you're not here."

"Did you hear what I said?"

He looked up at her. "No." His gaze returned to

Sunny who'd already started to purr. "It's amazing how she responds to you."

Erin grabbed his chin. "Focus."

"On what?"

"I'm talking about you intimidating Trent."

He sniffed amused. "No one could intimidate Trent."

"But you did."

He turned to her surprised. "No, I didn't."

"Yes, you did," she insisted. "He was...different. Tell me everything you said to him."

"You heard everything I said."

"Not when Mindy, Tara and I came here to see Sunny. I left you alone with him in my apartment. What did you say? You're lucky today was pretty average for me. There was an older man with abominable pain, which was bad but we were able to uncover the cause and another young man with a history of migraines came in complaining of a headache—"

"What does this have to do with anything?"

"In between all the patients I kept wondering what you must have said to Trent and silently wondered what kind of torture I'd have to use to make you confess."

Brandon sighed. "I'm sorry, but I don't know what you're talking about."

Erin clasped her hands together and said with feeling, "I really like him. I want this to work. He's not perfect but neither am I."

"He's not going to dump you."

"How do you know that?"

"Because I saw him—"

"You saw him what?" she pressed when he stopped.

Brandon scratched the back of his neck. "Eat your tart like a man who planned to stick around for a long time."

Erin frowned. "That doesn't make any sense."

"Trust me. You don't have to worry about him."

Erin covered her face and groaned.

"Now what?"

She let her hands fall to her lap. "If it's not you, then it's me. I did something wrong. I really wanted to blame you. I don't know what I said, but I upset him."

Brandon rested a hand on her shoulder. "You're over-thinking this."

"He wanted to tell me something."

"Then you should have listened to him."

"I didn't want to listen. He had that tone."

"What tone?"

"The 'It's not working' tone. The 'I'm tired of this and let's give each other some space' tone."

"So what?"

Erin's voice cracked. "So what?"

"Maybe you do need space. Maybe you need to see him in another light."

"I don't want to."

Brandon sent her a long look then said, "One day you're going to have to."

CHAPTER 32

She was fire.

Vince stood in the parking lot of Treeline Hospital and half expected the autumn leaves to burst into flames as he watched an attractive black woman with a short afro and confident walk, head towards a sleek black motorcycle.

She wasn't anything he'd imagined. No wonder Trent had changed, she was nothing like the women he'd dated in the past. She was like a wild horse that had never been broken. A challenge. A fascinating, sexy, challenge.

"Can I help you?"

Vince blinked. He'd been so busy studying her that he hadn't noticed that she'd walked past the motorcycle right up to him.

"You're just standing there," she continued, her sharp brown gaze assessing him. "Are you lost? Are you waiting for someone? Do you need assistance? Do you speak English? Which is a silly question because if you didn't you wouldn't know anything I just said, but—" She paused and slowed her pace. She tapped her chest. "I am a doctor."

"Are you Dr. Freeman?"

She stared. He wasn't sure if she was shocked because he knew her name or because he spoke perfect American English.

He cleared his throat. "Are you Dr. Erin Freeman?"

"Yes," she said recovering herself. "I am and I hope I didn't offend you by—"

"It's okay. Just don't start speaking to me in Korean or make any references."

She frowned. "I'm sorry?"

"Never mind."

"I think I do know a few Korean words if—"

"I'm not Korean."

"Oh. I thought so."

He paused. "You can tell?"

She looked a little embarrassed. "Well...not really. It's only that you remind me of someone."

Vince folded his arms ready to hate her. He'd been distracted by her appearance but now remembered why he was there. She was the reason Trent had changed. She was the enemy. If she mentioned the bands BTS or BigBang he'd hate her for life. "Who is that?"

"It was a while back. A guy named Vince Tran."

He stared at her, his arms falling to his sides. "What?"

Erin pulled out her cell phone. "You probably don't know who he is." She showed him an album cover on her screen: A black and white image of him with a shadow of an ax across his bare chest, his dragon tattoo illuminated in red. She shook her head. "This was years ago, but the resemblance is amazing."

This wasn't real. Nobody in the US knew who he was. It had been his secret pain that despite his success abroad no one stateside knew who he was and here was this stranger who recognized him? Had listened to his music? Had liked it? "How would you know Vince Tran?"

"So you *do* know who he is?"

"Hmm."

"I love his music, his songs. He talked about life, he talked about pain, and his looks, I mean, his hooks," she said quickly correcting herself, "were incredible. His music got me through medical school. I hadn't heard about him until I visited an aunt in Jamaica and my cousin attended his concert. She said his show was amazing, and came back with a CD. We played it over and over."

Vince was so happy he could cry. In one moment she'd made all his struggles and effort worth it—leaving school at seventeen, to his parent's horror; following his dream to become a singer/songwriter and traveling the world. It hadn't been easy. He hadn't soared the way he'd hoped. But if he hadn't followed his heart his life wouldn't be what it was now. He wouldn't have met his wife, had his son, met Trent or had his business. No, he hadn't become the international icon of his childhood fantasies, but he hadn't ended up working in a job he hated wondering "what might have been" either. He had been successful enough to buy a home and own his own prosperous recording studio. This stranger had made his life come full circle in perfect balance.

He swore. The enemy had won.

Her face began to change and she looked at him with awe. "It's you, isn't it?"

Vince nodded and she grinned. He swore. Did she have to be so pretty?

"I'm a grown woman so I'm not going to go fangirl on you, but—"

"You want an autograph?"

"No, a picture." Erin motioned him closer. "Please."

Vince stood beside her. She held out her phone and took a quick photo then looked at her work and wiggled her shoulders. "Ooh, my cousin's going to be so jealous."

"Dr. Freeman—"

"Just one minute," she said, typing something into her phone. "I've got to share this moment before it's over. And now... it's gone." She put the phone away. "What was it you wanted?"

I wanted to get rid of you. I wanted to find out what crazy hold you have on my friend and break the spell, but now I'm under it. He needed more time to think. She'd surprised him and he needed time to figure out what to do. Vince hesitated about telling her that he was Trent's friend. He didn't want her to think he was checking her out. He chose a more neutral introduction. "I'm...Cathy Lee's cousin-in-law. I wanted to meet you and thank you."

Erin's face lit up and Vince could see why Trent had fallen for her. Her smile was warm and genuine. "Thank you," she said. "But I didn't really do anything out of the ordinary. How is she by the way?"

"Still adjusting."

She nodded and her sweet brown gaze held his. "If she has any questions, I'm not an expert, but—"

"Right, sure. Thanks." Vince took a step back. He had to get away from her, resisting the fire of her pull. The heat and energy of her threatened to scorch him. "I don't want to take up any more of your time."

"It was great meeting you."

He waved and walked into the hospital even though that was the last place he wanted to be. He stopped in the main entrance before he turned and watched her climb onto her motorcycle and speed away. Trent had got himself an amazing woman. Getting him away from her wouldn't be easy and after meeting her, he wasn't sure he wanted to. She didn't seem that bad. Maybe Trent was changing on his own.

"Vincent?"

Vince briefly closed his eyes and silently swore. Only three people called him that: His mother, his grandmother and Trent's mother, Dr. Lorraine Brewster. He turned and saw the attractive older woman, her hair perfectly pulled back, sweeping her shoulders. She had a cold beauty, a fierce intellect and a voice that made him think of frosted mountain tops, even when she was trying to be friendly like now. "I thought it was you. What are you doing here?"

And Vince, like a kid caught by a strict headmistress, said four words he would regret.

CHAPTER 33

"You said what!"

"I'm sorry," Vince said sounding miserable. He faced Trent's desk in the SonTil Sounds office. He glanced at a large black and emerald green poster of a sound wave spreading along the side wall, feeling as if he'd been hit by a sonic boom. He knew he could have sent Trent a text, but he thought he owed it to his friend to give him the bad news in person. "I really didn't mean this to happen, but your mother..." He shook his head. "She caught me off guard. I was still recovering from being recognized and—"

Trent stood behind his desk and tapped it with his finger. "You told my mother you were visiting my girlfriend?"

Vince pressed his hands together. "I'm truly sorry."

"And you gave my mother her name. Her *full* name?"

He shrugged. "She asked."

Trent slowly came from behind the desk, his eyes

dark. "And now she wants to gather the vipers together to meet her."

Vince cleared his throat. "You shouldn't talk about your family like that."

"I was being generous."

Vince sat and lowered his gaze no longer able to meet Trent's. "It won't be so bad. All your other girlfriends survived."

"Erin was never supposed to meet them."

His head shot up. "Why not?"

"I was going to break up with her."

Vince surged to his feet. "Why didn't you tell me that?"

"I didn't think I had to."

He frantically looked around the room for a reason to change the subject. "Do you still serve coffee that tastes like s—"

"I told you to stay away."

"I was curious alright? I wanted to meet the woman who turned you into this." He gestured to Trent's dark trousers and sleek wine colored shirt.

Trent returned to his desk.

"What's going on?"

Trent sat behind his desk and clasped his hands together.

Vince knew his friend too well to be intimidated. "She's great and she's good for you."

"You only think that because she flattered you, K-Pop."

Vince flashed him a rude gesture. Trent sent him one in return.

Vince sighed and sat. "I don't know what's going on, but I think if you told me I could help and—"

"Do you know the difference between noise and sound?" Trent didn't give Vince the chance to respond. "Sound is something pleasant that we hear, while noise is unpleasant or rather unwanted sound. Right now you're making noise." He motioned to the door. "I need to figure out how to fix this disaster."

"She's a doctor. She'll fit in with your family." Vince paused and leaned back when Trent sent him a look. He finally understood.

Trent nodded. "That's what I'm afraid of."

***

The Brewster's didn't have family dinners.

They had appointments.

So on Erin's day off she was scheduled to have an early lunch with his mother, a midday coffee with his sister and dinner with his father. (Thankfully his two stepmothers were busy otherwise their curiosity would have been added to the mix) Trent knew his family would do a quick, clean dissection of her and he wasn't disappointed.

His mother, with her superior tone and keen intellect, dissected Erin's background asking about her family and schooling making it appear more of an interview than an interrogation. His sister, Ana, with her soft voice and haunted eyes, asked Erin about her present situation and workload. His sister's questions were pointed and polite and after Ana had left the cafe, Erin mentioned that she liked her but wondered about her sad eyes. Trent noticed them too, always had, even when she was younger, but brushed over Erin's observation and changed the subject.

Now he had to face the final battle.

Trent anticipated and dreaded the last dissection with his father. He knew he would be all about the future. A dangerous topic that still caused tension between him and his father. He had to be on guard. Trent stood in front of his father's colonial, in a zip code known for private schools, Ivy League graduates and grocery stores that carried fifteen dollar bottled juices, and rang the doorbell.

"You being nervous is making me nervous," Erin said.

Trent tugged his collar. The autumn air was chilly but he felt warm. "I'm not nervous." He glanced down at what was in her hand. "And you didn't need to buy a basket of fruit."

"I couldn't come empty handed."

"It's the size of a suitcase. Was the hospital gift shop having a sale?" She'd given similar, yet smaller gifts to his mother and sister. He knew his mother would hand it over to her maid and his sister would eat some alone in her office.

The door swung open, bathing them in light and stopping her reply.

Xavier stood there with a wide grin. "Come in. Let me take your coats."

Erin handed him her coat then said in a teasing voice, "Surprised to see me?"

He winked. "I knew I would."

"I didn't."

His gaze slowly trailed the length of her blue wrap dress. "And I must say what I see is very—"

Trent cleared his throat.

"Nice," Xavier finished. He pointed down the hall. "Head down there then make a right."

She nodded before she left.

"What are you doing here?" Trent demanded in a low voice.

Xavier's grin turned naughty as he opened up the closet. "You think I'd miss this?"

———

She was prepared for a shark. What she met was a teddy bear: Handsome, but not intimidating; tall but not overbearingly so, sweet and harmless. At least that's what Erin thought of Trent's father at first. He shook her hand and had an easy smile that put her at ease. He was nothing like his son Xavier and reminded her more of Trent until his gaze fixated on her. That's when she saw a predator.

And she was prey.

"So Trent tells me you work in the ER," Dr. Steven Brewster said halfway through the dinner of red beans and rice with vegetable roti following banal pleasantries. Xavier sat opposite Trent and Erin while Dr. Brewster sat at the head of the table.

"Yes."

"When do you plan on selecting a specialty?"

"I don't plan to. I like working in the ER. I like

thinking that I'm a specialist in everything for the first five minutes." She laughed.

No one else did.

"You're not thinking long-term. There's more money in—"

"I know but I didn't become a doctor for the money."

Silence.

Trent finally spoke up. "Dad, she—"

His father leaned forward. "Don't you want to make a difference?"

"I feel I am making a difference," Erin said.

"In a reactionary way, but true change happens with dedicated attention to a particular problem. I'm sure you have a fine mind—"

"That I use to help the patients who see me."

"And who quickly forget you."

Erin shrugged unfazed. "As long as they're okay, that's fine with me."

"Do you want to have a family?"

"Of course."

Dr. Brewster sniffed and shook his head. "There's no 'of course' about it. You'd need a very understanding spouse to accept your debt and your schedule." He shot Trent a look. "Which I bet is why you chose him. He's as soft as—"

"Dad—" Trent cut in afraid his father would reveal too much.

"ER doctors have married and had children in the past so I wouldn't be the first," Erin said.

"Did Trent tell you that he hates doctors?" Xavier said.

Trent glared at him; Xavier grinned. "Clearly not."

"Why would he tell me something that isn't true?" Erin said. "He wouldn't have developed the OnTheSpot device if he did."

Dr. Brewster and Xavier shared a look.

Erin looked at them confused. "What?"

"He developed that to help nurses not doctors," Dr. Brewster clarified.

"Oh, well...I'm glad I changed his mind about doctors then."

Dr. Brewster looked at her amused. "That's yet to be seen."

Erin stiffened, hating his patronizing look. "When we're alone together I see it quite clearly actually. Feel it too."

Xavier laughed.

Erin blushed horrified. "I didn't mean it like that."

"You made your point," Dr. Brewster said.

"Point. I'm sure it was a hard one," Xavier said then laughed harder.

"I don't hate doctors anymore," Trent said. He glared at his brother. "Just one."

Dr. Brewster nodded surprised. "So you stopped blaming us for Maya's—"

Trent cut him off and said in a dark tone, "We agreed never to talk about that again."

"You made that decision for the rest of us. Ana—"

"I did it for Ana. I look after her since her father won't."

Dr. Brewster held his son's gaze then turned with irritation to Xavier who was still laughing. "That's enough. You get far too much enjoyment stirring up trouble."

Xavier bit his lip and lowered his head. "Sorry."

He turned his attention to Erin. "If you manage to stay around I won't stop trying to persuade you to better yourself. Especially if you plan to stay with him." He looked at Trent. "You know what's involved. Would you give up everything for her?"

"Of course he wouldn't," Erin said, surprised by the question. "You don't know your son very well if you think he'd give up anything for me. He's not that kind of man."

Dr. Brewster kept his gaze on Trent and lifted a questioning brow. "Is that right?"

Erin couldn't understand the disbelief in the older man's tone. "Yes."

Dr. Brewster switched his gaze to her face and smiled a secretive smile. "Then you're right. I don't know my son as well as I thought."

PLEASE DON'T ASK ABOUT MAYA. PLEASE DON'T ASK *about Maya.* That was all Trent could repeat as he drove Erin home that evening. His father had been careless mentioning her and he wasn't in the mood for questions. Erin sat silently beside him, which was rare, and he could imagine her mind swirling with questions to ask him. He'd have to be strategic in deflecting or avoiding them.

"Is it true that you hate doctors?" Erin finally asked him.

Trent felt his tension ebb. This was a question he

could answer, if not fully. *Yes, and I have my reasons.* "Let's just say that I was biased before I met you."

"How did I change your mind?"

He couldn't stop a smile. "Who said you changed my mind?"

She playfully punched him. "Be serious."

He couldn't be. It hurt too much. He didn't want to remember the moment when she asked about Cathy and bought the book for them to read. He didn't want to remember sitting on the couch beside her with Roger at their feet while she read passages from the book and he watched her mouth move when he should have been listening. He didn't want to remember the exact moment he realized she was different than any doctor he'd ever met. Any woman, for that matter.

"Fishing for a compliment?" he said.

"No, I'm really curious."

He pretended to think for a moment then shook his head. "I don't know."

CHAPTER 34

"I scheduled a bus tour around the city," Erin said as they exited Union Station in downtown DC. He and Erin had taken the metro into the city for the day. The pavement was crowded with a mixture of tourists, locals and working professionals.

Trent shook his head as they headed for the street, fear crawling up his neck like an army of fire ants. "I don't do buses."

"Why not?"

"Just not my thing."

"Come on. It will be fun to try something different." She took his hand, desperate not to lose him, in more ways than one. It had been a week since she'd met Trent's family and he seemed more distant than before. She wanted to find a way to reconnect with him and had hoped the bus trip would be just the thing. When the city tour bus arrived she led him to a seat. But within minutes she knew something was wrong. He didn't seem to be listening to the announcer and she saw a sheen of sweat on his forehead. "What's wrong?" she asked in a low voice.

"We have to get off at the next stop."

She was about to argue, but the tone of his voice and the look on his face warned her not to. At the next stop they got off near the Tidal Basin.

He wiped his forehead and looked out at the partially man-made reservoir that seemed to shimmer under an orange sun. "Don't plan things like this without telling me first."

"I thought it would be a nice surprise."

"I don't like buses."

"Why not?"

He turned his gaze to the cherry trees surrounding the Tidal Basin painted in shades of green, red and yellow their colors reflecting in the water. "Doesn't matter."

"Is it a phobia or something?"

His tone turned hard. "I said it doesn't matter."

"It's not something to be ashamed of, but—"

"Erin. It. Doesn't. Matter."

"It matters to me," she shot back. "I want to understand. You don't know what it's like trying to guess whether I'll offend you or not because you won't tell me anything."

"I tell you plenty."

"Only what you want me to know."

"If you don't like it then..."

She nodded. "I was waiting for when that ultimatum

would come." She folded her arms. "Did I give you the excuse you needed?"

"Excuse?"

"Yes, to dump me."

He sighed and turned away.

"Go on. I'm ready."

"That's not it."

"Then what is it? I know I sometimes ask a lot of questions, but I think I should know if my boyfriend is going to have a panic attack on a bus."

He gripped his hand into a fist. "It wasn't that bad."

She began counting items off on her fingers. "Increased pulse, shallow breathing, constricted pupils—"

"You think it's funny?"

"Am I laughing?"

Trent shoved his hands in his pockets. "There's nothing wrong with me. If you want to finish the stupid bus tour we can."

"That's not the point." Erin sighed, shook her head and held her hands up in surrender. "You win. I'm done."

"What?"

"I'm sick of trying to figure you out."

His brows shot up. "Oh really? I thought you liked me the way I am."

"That's not fair."

"What's not fair is you bitching about—"

"Bitching? Really? Do you hear yourself?" She shook her head. "It's times like these that... One moment you seem one way and the next...it's like you're somebody else. Sometimes I think you like me, but then I'm not sure." She took a deep breath. "Why won't you talk to me?"

"I talk to you."

"About important things."

"Like what?"

"Like why you were surprised when I asked about Cathy? Why you were shocked I was upset watching you flirt with another woman? Why did my brother bother you so much? Why does your father hardly know you and why you nearly ran to get off of a stupid bus!"

"I don't know."

Erin looked sad. "Yes, you do. You just don't want to tell me. And I understand. I think we need to give each other some space."

She turned and walked away.

CHAPTER 35

She was leaving. Trent watched her bright red coat grow distant in the sparse crowd.

Keeping her in the dark was supposed to be part of his charm. But lately he'd felt as if all his past charm had left him completely. He couldn't hold up. He couldn't be the man she wanted and this trip had proven it. He could fake everything else; the attitude, the clothes, the walk. But the old Trent and the new Trent had the same phobia—buses. He hadn't managed to get over it yet.

He leaned against the railing that snaked around the reservoir, lowered his head and closed his eyes. He couldn't watch her walk away and he couldn't go after her. He had to let her leave, it was his only way out. At least it was a clean break. There would be no tears. No light touches on his arms and a "Let's be friends". She'd disappear from his life forever. He listened to the sound of a slight breeze sweeping over the water and the wheels of a push chair and a child's giggle. His throat closed, he'd never be behind one with her.

But that was fine. He'd move on. It wasn't meant to last. Trent opened his eyes and saw purple and black sneakers.

Her sneakers.

She'd come back.

His heart began to pound. He didn't dare raise his head in case his happiness showed on his face. He had to remain cool. Nonchalant.

"Trent?"

"Hmm?"

He felt her fingertips against his scar. He should have pulled away, but he didn't. He closed his eyes and listened to the wind, the tires against the road, a car door closing.

"How old were you when the bus crashed?"

She knew even though he hadn't told her. He could lie, but he didn't want to. He kept his eyes closed. "Seventeen."

"I'm sorry."

He lifted his head and looked at her, disgusted with himself. "Don't be. I should be over it by now."

But looking at her was a mistake because the compassion in her eyes was nearly his undoing. She took his hand. "Just the thought makes your hands clammy."

Trent tried to pull his hand away, but she kept her grip. "It's okay. I don't mind." She was quiet a moment then said, "How about we get off at each stop along the bus route?"

"It would take us forever."

"But we'd get to finish the tour and you'd see that the bus is safe."

"No."

"Let's give it a try at one stop then."

He hated her seeing how vulnerable he was. But he could manage one short distance. "Fine."

It wasn't easy, but he was willing. He had to conquer this.

Unfortunately, the moment he was on the bus and heard the air brakes, hissing like a snake, and felt the bus shift to one side like a giant creature rising up as it made its way between the smaller cars his heart raced, his skin felt damp, and he counted until they could get off again.

"Close your eyes," Erin said before she covered his ears. He didn't ask her why and it seemed to help.

They didn't speak again—to his relief—until they were safely far away from any buses and riding the metro back to where they'd parked their car. Once he'd fully recovered he said, "Why did you cover my ears like that?"

"I think it's the sound that bothers you the most. It's what triggers the memory for you. You were better the second time around."

"Maybe but I'm not cured."

"I know."

"But thanks for trying."

"Thanks for trusting me."

He paused. He'd never thought of it that way. She'd been upset because she didn't feel he trusted her. She was right. He didn't. He couldn't. He still had to be careful what he revealed or risk losing her. But he was glad with the risk he'd taken. At least she knew this much about him and it hadn't been as bad as he'd thought. She didn't laugh at him or try to analyze him. She was really curious. Not because she saw him as a specimen or a patient but because she cared. *I want to know if my boyfriend is going to have a panic attack on a bus.* Her boyfriend. She made it seem reasonable that she'd worry about him. His parents hadn't. She didn't seem embarrassed but truly worried. It was a strange feeling.

"Why did you choose medicine?" he asked her as the metro hummed to a stop at a station.

"It chose me."

He'd never heard that before. "How?"

"Somehow, since a little girl, I knew what I wanted to do. I liked the thought of being a doctor and helping people. It's strange. I can't pinpoint a moment where I can connect the feeling. I just knew. Some people see a teacher or a police officer or a chef and say "I want to do that". I saw a doctor somewhere whether on TV or in a magazine or book but somewhere and thought 'I want to do that' and never changed. My family wasn't sure I was serious because lots of kids say they want this path, but I never wavered. They said I was always bandaging up my dolls and my brother's toys. I had my little hospital where I would fix them up.

"When I was a little older I toyed with the idea of being a vet, but soon realized I liked helping people. But I did briefly volunteer at an animal shelter because I liked animals and read about a woman working with stray animals who needed help. I always liked to help so I gave my time there for a few summers and after school."

Trent briefly saw her through his father's eyes. He

knew as an ER doctor at a small, local hospital she wasn't making big money so she couldn't have gone into the field for that. And the prestige wasn't there either. The emergency department was a hard choice and the burnout rate high. But when she talked about her work she seemed happy. She saw it as a calling. That was something his family could never understand. But he did. He understood it completely. If only she could understand him just as much.

Erin lowered her head and rubbed her hands together. "I know you still want space."

Trent stared out the window as the light from the day was swallowed up by darkness as the metro entered a tunnel "Erin, I'm fine."

She continued as if he hadn't spoken. "And I'm going to give it to you. I'm going away."

He turned sharply to her. "No."

"It's already planned."

Play it cool. Play it cool. Don't let her know how much this hurts. "Where are you going?"

"A trip to Haiti. It's a medical exchange program. I've been planning for years. I'll be gone for almost two weeks." She playfully nudged him. "You'd better miss me."

CHAPTER 36

He more than missed her.

He felt like he was coming down with something. He was tired. Weary. He missed her so much and it hurt that he couldn't do anything about it. Trent lay on his couch with Roger, a heavy warm weigh curled up at his feet.

Her absence made his place feel like more of a façade than it already was, his clothes like costumes. His furniture was stylish but uncomfortable and without Erin's soft body next to him his couch felt like a board.

The old Trent would have texted her to make sure she'd arrived safe; checked in a couple days later to make sure she was taking care of herself then later sent a picture with an image of a stuffed bear with a bandage over its heart. But the new Trent didn't care. The new Trent knew she'd come back in a few days and had to act like it was expected.

The new Trent was killing him.

You're pathetic. He could hear his brother telling him. *You shouldn't care about a woman this much. This is why they walk all over you.* Even at work his colleagues saw the change in him but knew better than to say anything. He was cold and detached. This is what control looked like. She could have sent something to him. His brother had once gotten a picture of black lace panties. He doubted Erin would send him that. So far she hadn't sent him anything. Probably too busy.

Trent stared at his quiet phone. He'd put it on the ground beside him, willing it to do something. But it mocked him instead. Its silence a punishment for his foolish hopes.

He picked it up. A text wouldn't be cheating, would it? The new Trent could offer a quick "Hello. Hope you're okay."

She'd say she was fine and that would be it. He started to text then stopped and deleted the message. He'd see her soon. A couple more days. He could wait.

He had to wait.

And then when he saw her again he had to pretend that he didn't want to hold her close. That he didn't want to spend a string of days in bed with her. He'd play it cool. Take her out to dinner. Be casual. He buried his face in the cushion and groaned.

Pretending that he didn't want to be with her would be even harder than pretending he didn't miss her. He was in serious trouble. He squeezed his eyes shut, feeling the tiny pounding of an oncoming headache.

He called Mindy. "Could you walk Roger for me for a couple of days?"

"What's wrong?"

"I think I'm coming down with the flu."

"That's impossible. You're never sick. The entire population could come down with some alien virus and you'd still be immune."

"Is that a no?"

"What's wrong?"

He pinched the bridge of his nose. "I just told you."

"If you're really feeling bad perhaps you should go to the hospital. Maybe you need to see a doctor. An ER doctor."

"I'm hanging up now."

"Okay, okay I'll do it. Roger shouldn't suffer because his owner is crazy."

"Hmm."

"I think you're being unfair to her."

"She doesn't need another brother."

"What?"

"Never mind."

"You can't keep this up."

He disconnected and put the phone down with a sigh. "I know."

***

ROGER WAS NOT TOO PLEASED WITH MINDY'S WALKS. She didn't take him as far as he liked to go so on the third day when he returned home he showed his displeasure by peeing in the foyer and chewing up a rug. He was frustrated, but Trent stayed in bed too tired to deal with him. He'd hire a dog walker.

But Roger wasn't the only problem. Mindy had a habit of leaving a mess behind her. Trent heard her laughing in the living room and smelled the burnt remnants of the cheese and nachos she'd tried to make. Roger came into the bedroom and whined at him.

"Just one more day, buddy," Trent said, feeling as old as the earth. "I promise."

Roger made a low sound in his throat. Trent reached out and ruffled his soft, brown fur then patted him on the head. "Okay, I'll get rid of her tonight and give you a proper walk."

Trent didn't know how much longer he slept. But he got up and washed his face, grabbed a pair of jeans and his red Star Trek hoodie, which his brother had forced him to shove to the back of his closet. He'd be the old Trent for a day when no one was looking. He took Roger on their typical mile walk where Roger found a frog (they left it alone) and a baby's blue sock that Roger, for some reason, wanted to keep as a souvenir.

Trent inhaled the chilled air feeling the coming of winter. He could make this work. The time away from Erin had helped him assess what mattered to him.

He didn't want a life without her.

He returned home (surprised that Roger seemed oddly excited to do so) relieved and surprised that the burnt smell had gone. He collapsed on the couch. Instead of reviving him the walk made him feel even more tired than before, but at least Roger was happy. Trent heard the dog's footsteps against the hardwood floor as he went to add the sock to his favorite pile of discoveries then he heard him in the kitchen (nosier than usual) as he lapped up water from his bowl before he settled in front of the window.

Trent closed his eyes and drifted off to sleep.

He slowly woke to the sound of Mindy's voice. "You can't keep this up," she scolded him. He felt her cool fingers against his cheek. Funny she'd never done that before.

"I told you that I have to," he said. "I don't have a choice."

"Of course you have a choice." Her voice was soft, softer than it had ever been before, her fingers making him relax. It shouldn't feel this good. He must be worse off than he thought.

"You know better than anyone that I don't have a choice. At least not the one I want."

"If you'd let me help you—"

"You've helped enough. Thanks."

"I didn't do much. Just cleaned a few dishes. One I had to soak because whatever was burnt on it stuck tight."

Trent paused. Mindy didn't clean. Mindy *never* cleaned. His eyes flew open as another realization hit him. She also didn't talk softly to him or stroke his cheek like this. Which could only mean...

He jumped to his feet, heard a gasp of surprise. He stared at her with his mouth open, his heart pounding so loud he couldn't hear anything else. Erin. He had been talking to Erin. Not Mindy. He glanced down at his clothes and silently swore. He was wearing a Star Trek hoodie! The one from the movie The Wrath of Khan. Why hadn't he chosen his Next Generation or Enterprise, one that looked a little less showy? Why had he chosen it at all? His brother was right. He should have gotten rid of them.

And God...what had he told her? Trent frantically searched his mind. He thought he was vague, but he could have revealed everything and ruined it all. Damn Mindy! He pulled out his cell phone. Not one message. She should have at least warned him. He glanced up and saw Erin's face. She looked frightened. "What's wrong?" he demanded.

"You tell me. You're the one who's angry."

Trent ran a hand down his face. Yes, he was, but not with her. He didn't mean to frighten her. "I didn't expect you back yet."

"I returned a day earlier. I was going to let you know then Mindy called me. She said you were sick and needed someone to look after Roger. She gave me your key. When I got here you had gone for your walk, but the place was a mess and...did I do something wrong?"

He sat down, rested his head on her lap and closed his eyes. It was so good to see her again. She was home. "No. I was startled, that's all."

"Clearly." She pressed the back of her hand against the side of his neck. "You did feel a little warm before."

"I'm fine now that you're—" He bit his lip. *Keep it cool.* "The one who cleaned up things. Thanks. Mindy can be a mess."

"No kidding."

He folded his arms. "How was your trip?"

"Tiring but invigorating and I missed you."

"Hmm...same." He sat up ready to look at her

without revealing his feelings. "You didn't have to come by. Mindy shouldn't have told you—"

Erin pressed a finger over his mouth. "I'm glad she did. It's nice to look after the man I love."

He stopped breathing. Love. She said she loved him. He was usually the first one to say it. No one had ever said it to him first. His strategy had worked. But the problem was, as he looked into her eyes, as he felt the pressure of her finger against his lips, he realized he loved her back. And he couldn't tell her because he knew she didn't really love him. She loved the new Trent. Not the *real* Trent. He wasn't sure who that was anymore.

Erin stood. "Would you like something to eat?"

"No," he said in a hoarse voice. "But thanks." He cleared his throat. "Nice to have you back."

"Nice to be back." She disappeared into the kitchen.

Trent squeezed his eyes shut and held his head. What did he do now? He should break up with her now before he became more attached. He swore. He was already in love with her how much more attached could he be? But he could stop himself from falling further. He had to. He needed to give himself a break. He'd proven his theory and now it was time to stay away from women like her.

He heard her footsteps, a sharp intake of breath, plates clattering on the coffee table, before she fell on the couch beside him and gathered him in her arms. "What on earth is wrong? Do you need a bucket?"

"No, why?"

"You look like you're going to be sick."

He already felt sick. He licked his lip and swallowed.

"Think you can make it to the sink?"

He shook his head. "I'm not—"

Erin jumped to her feet, but Trent grabbed her hand before she could leave to search for something. "I'm not going to be sick."

Her eyes scanned his face. "Yes, your color is coming back." She rested a hand on her chest and took a deep breath. "You scared me for a minute. But you still look miserable."

He looked away. "Don't say you love me."

She blinked. "Is that what made you ill?"

"Yes, but not for the reason you think. I..."

"I didn't say it to burden you or anything. I only wanted you to know how I feel." She smiled but it was sad. "I didn't expect it to make you sick."

Would you still love me if you knew how much I missed you? How much I thought of you? How much I want to hold you right now?

Her expression changed. "You want to break up with me, don't you? You feel pressured, cornered and—"

His mouth covered hers and she tasted better than he'd remembered. And not only had she stolen his heart, she was like a drug. He was addicted to her attention. No one had cared about him the way she did. Even as a child he'd been forced to go to school in agony, it was only when he'd collapsed in the cafeteria and rushed to the hospital because of a burst appendix that his parents— briefly—paid any attention to him. No former girlfriend had ever treated him the way Erin did. He wasn't going back. He had her love now. He would bury the old Trent forever.

Erin drew back and laughed. "Well, that was the kind of welcome I was hoping for."

"Good." He gathered her close and his voice deepened. "I plan to do a lot more."

"I wish I could, but I'm tired after cleaning up."

Damn. "I know. Mindy likes to leave a mess."

Erin paused. "Yes, that's what I thought you said. But at my place I thought you said she liked to keep things tidy. That she fixed up my place."

Trent hesitated remembering that lie. "Yes...well."

She studied his face then said, "You did it, didn't you? You cleaned up my place."

He stood, her words arousing his fears. He was too close to having all that he wanted. He couldn't lose it now.

"Why did you lie?"

He rested his hands on his hips and faced her. "I didn't want you to think it was a habit."

Erin looked up at him confused. "Why would I think that?"

The doorbell saved him from answering.

CHAPTER 37

He opened the door to a nightmare.

Dorothy stood there, her eyes heavy—evidence of having a little too much to drink, but not enough to be plastered. She always did impulsive things when she was in that mood.

She stumbled inside. "Derrick and I had a fight." She walked past him to the living room. "I had a few drinks, don't worry I didn't drive, I just didn't want to go home and I didn't know where else to go."

"I'm—"

She stopped when she saw Erin sitting on the couch. "Oh. You have company." She giggled. "That's rare."

He swore. If he didn't get rid of her soon, she'd blow his cover. He didn't want Erin to know that he usually spent the nights alone. That he hadn't had hordes of girlfriends. "We can talk later. Let me get you a—"

Dorothy looked around the room with a frown on her

face. "What's going on here? Are you moving or something? Your place looks different."

"It's fine. Now—"

"Do you even live here anymore? It doesn't look like you at all. Are you renting it out to someone?"

He gently took her arm. "No."

She pointed to a wall. "But you used to have the Broadway poster for *Hamilton* over there."

Trent felt his face burn. The next thing she'd share was that he had the entire score memorized. "Dorothy, you should—"

She looked at him. "At least you haven't changed your clothes. You're still wearing that Star Wars—"

"Star Trek."

"Hoodie."

Trent pulled her towards the front door. "Right, the one you hated and now don't have to worry about anymore."

Dorothy yanked her arm free and narrowed her eyes at Erin. "How come you look familiar?"

"We met at your wedding," Erin said. "I'm Derrick's cousin."

"Oh." She laughed. "Then I'd better watch what I have to say."

Trent cleared his throat. "Dorothy, this isn't the time."

She looked at the empty plates left on the coffee table. "Oh, did Trent make something for you?"

Erin sniffed. "Trent doesn't cook."

"Doesn't cook?" Dorothy turned to Trent surprised. "You haven't even made her Johnny cakes and codfish?

Why are you lying to her?" She looked at Erin with a little pity. "You should have seen the meal he prepared for me on our—"

"That's enough."

Erin stood. "I can come back."

Trent whistled and Roger came running. "Take him on a quick stroll. A couple minutes."

She hesitated then nodded and grabbed his leash from the hall.

Once he heard the front door close, Trent turned to Dorothy exasperated. "What is wrong with you?"

"Me?" she said shocked. "What happened to you?" She looked around the room again. "This place is amazing."

"Answer my question."

"I told you why I'm here."

"You can't come over without calling first."

She sat down and folded her arms. "I could before."

"You weren't a married woman before."

She bounced up and down on the sofa then ran her hand over the cushion. "This material is incredible. I'm so glad you got rid of that other one."

"Dorothy—"

She stood and looked at one of the paintings. "When did you start seeing her? Why did you lie about cooking?"

"You need to go home."

She spun around. "I haven't heard from you in awhile. Have you been avoiding me?"

"I've been busy."

"You used to always make time for me. I thought we were friends."

He sighed. "We are."

"I thought you cared about me."

"How much did you have to drink?"

"Not enough." Her face crumbled. "I really believed you when you said you loved me."

"What?"

"But you didn't."

"What are you talking about?"

She stretched her arms out to indicate the room. "Why didn't you do this for me? Why didn't you change for me? If this is who you are, why did you hide it? I never knew you could be like this—so sexy and funny."

Trent tugged on his hoodie shocked. "You call this sexy?"

"No, but when you were at my place you were different and even at the wedding and you did this all for her."

"It's not that simple."

"It is. If you'd truly loved me you would have changed."

"If you truly loved me I wouldn't have had to."

Dorothy folded her arms. "So what makes her so special? I'm curious. I may not have loved you as you were before but I liked you. Can you say the same thing about her? What will happen when she finds out the real you?"

Dorothy still mattered too much to him, that's why her words seared his heart. Erin loved a fraud. A false man. Why hadn't he changed for Dorothy? He could have tried to win her back by trying to be the man Derrick was. Why had he let her go?

Because loving her hurt. It came with a price. He hadn't seen it before, but he saw it now. "You need to go."

"I lied."

"What?"

She crossed the distance between them and touched his face. She smelled of a sweet white wine and violets. Wilted violets. "I didn't come here because of Derrick. It's because I miss you. I miss our friendship."

He should have moved away, but didn't. He rested his hands on her shoulders and softened his voice. For the first time his heart moved from pity not longing. "I told you we're still friends."

"But I want you to keep loving me the way you used to. I know it sounds selfish, but it's how I feel. I'm so used to you always being there for me and now I feel lost without my best friend."

"I'm not the man I used to be. I want more. It wasn't that I didn't love you enough, you couldn't love me enough."

She tenderly cupped his face in a way he'd always wanted her to. "I don't want to lose our friendship."

He turned his face away and said in a low, tight voice, "Stop it."

"What?"

"Stop pretending that you don't know that I still love you."

He paused when he heard a sound. A sound that filled him with dread: Roger's dog collar. He turned and saw Erin standing in the entryway.

CHAPTER 38

She didn't look angry. Just shocked and hurt. "You told me to come back in a couple minutes," she said. "But I think—"

"No, come in. Dorothy's leaving." He took Dorothy's arm and led her outside, pulled out his cell phone and called her a ride.

"It's chilly out here," she said, rubbing her arms.

He looked at her thick suede coat. "I know."

"Couldn't we wait in the foyer?"

He stared out at the street. "No."

She lowered her head. "I didn't mean to cause trouble."

"Yes, you did."

She looked at him. "I really do miss you."

He sighed and turned to her. "No, you miss having my attention. Not me. And I lied too."

"About what?"

He held her gaze. "I can't be friends."

She sniffed unconvinced. "You don't mean that. We can go back to—"

"There's nothing to go back to. And I'm not saying this because I still love you, it's because I realize that you don't understand me any better than Erin does."

"At least I know the real you."

He nodded. "And it wasn't until this moment that I saw that you never liked him. But I amused you until someone better came along. I know what you've told others about me behind my back. I was your friend but you were never mine." Trent turned and went back inside, closing the door in her face. His legs felt heavy as he made his way to the living room. The expression that had been on Erin's face loomed large in his mind. *You didn't do anything wrong*, he could hear his brother say. *Don't explain anything.*

"You're still in love with her," Erin said when she saw him. "I heard you say it."

Trent didn't move. *Let her talk. Don't explain. Your past is none of her business.*

"Is that why you changed how you decorated your place? Too many memories of her?"

He sat on the couch. Roger, sensing something wrong, came and rested his head on Trent's knee. He quickly stroked him then motioned him to go.

Erin stood in front of him. "I always felt that you were keeping me at bay for a reason. That there was a part of you you were hiding. Is this it?"

He folded his arms. He had to put her on the offensive. He had to show her that he didn't care if she left or stayed. That was the only power he had. "What do you want me to say?"

"That I have a chance." He heard tears in her voice and saw them glistening in her eyes.

"What?"

"Do you think you could love me one day?"

Yes. I do if only I knew you could really love me too. "Erin I—"

"I know. Stupid question. I should have realized that guys like you only see women like me as friends. Good friends. Great friends. Friends with benefits. Safe. Nothing more. I know you need time and I'm willing to give it to you if...if I have a chance. But if not...then I should go."

His heart cracked a little. He knew exactly how she felt and couldn't tell her so. He never imagined that she had experienced what he had. What losers had been in her life? Who could have made her feel so unwanted?

He felt her pain. Then he felt his anger. Dorothy had no right to come into his life and pretend like nothing had changed. And he had loved her once. Still loved her, but not in the same way.

He didn't want Erin to go. He hated having to pretend, but she'd fallen for someone else. Someone he'd continue to strive to be if that meant he didn't have to lose her.

She lowered her head and moved towards the hall.

He rushed up and blocked her. "We dated for two years. It ended. We stayed friends. That's it. Dorothy invited herself over here. I didn't. I asked you to come back. If that doesn't show you who I'd prefer to be with then nothing will."

She kept her head lowered. "I'm ashamed."

"Why?"

"Because I'm still jealous."

Don't be. He wanted to tell her. He lifted her chin and kissed her instead, even though it felt inadequate. She was hurting and he was pushing her pain aside. He hated himself for it. But he didn't want to threaten what they had. The old Trent would have held her and told her about his broken heart, how she'd helped to heal him, how much he liked being with her. How much he wanted her to stay. But the new Trent didn't use words. He used his body. It was easier, quicker, faster and safer than exposing his heart.

He didn't dare do that. That had always been his downfall.

ERIN LAY IN BED AS TRENT SLEPT BESIDE HER. SHE had no right to be jealous. Trent was right. He was with her now. His past was his past. He didn't need to apologize or explain it. But she'd seen a different man. When he'd held Dorothy close she saw a tender, gentle loving man. He'd never held her like that. Looked at her like that. Even his voice was different. Softer somehow.

She'd seen and felt glimpses of it when he kissed her, when they were together in bed, but never outside of that. Erin pressed her hands over her eyes. What was she doing? Why was she trying to attain what she could never have? She should be satisfied. He treated her well. He was a great lover. So he never cooked for her. Did that matter?

Yes, her heart screamed. She didn't want to feel like a casual fling. She wanted to understand him completely. There were still so many questions. She'd gone away (and missed him miserably) and given him space. She didn't know what else to do.

Why couldn't she inspire passion in him? True desire? Even love? *Just take what you can get,* her mind told her. You're not the easiest woman to be with. Your schedule can be crazy, you can be overwhelming sometimes. Relax. Don't ruin a good thing.

"Erin?"

The sound of Trent's deep voice shocked her in the still darkness of the room. Her voice came out as a squeak. "Yes?"

"I don't love her anymore. Not like I used to." He pulled the blanket up to her shoulder. "Now go to sleep."

Her heart lifted. He was giving her a chance. He was letting her know she could win his heart. She smiled into the darkness. "I will."

***

SHE WOKE UP TO THE SOUND OF SOMETHING SIZZLING and the scent of mangoes and frying fish.

Erin walked into the kitchen amazed to see the ease with which Trent moved about. She sat at the kitchen table and watched him. All this time she'd thought he couldn't cook. Why had he kept that from her? He turned to her, briefly gave her a curt humorless "Morning" before setting a plate in front of her. She lowered her gaze and gasped at the sight of flat, fried dumplings. "Johnny cakes and codfish!"

"Hmm."

He placed a plate of mango slices beside her.

Her eyes filled with tears of joy. He'd cooked and made breakfast for her. No man she'd ever been with had done that for her. "Thank you."

Trent sat down and nodded, clearly not wanting her thanks.

"I really appreciate this," she said, wondering why he looked annoyed.

"Just eat it."

She nodded happily and dove in.

Trent silently watched her. Doing something like this was a risk, but he'd hardly been able to sleep after seeing her near tears last night. And looking at her beaming now made it all worth it. One slip-up wouldn't ruin everything. Besides, the Star Trek hoodie hadn't turned her off so maybe he could adjust his strategy a little.

"I don't know why you felt you had to hide this from me," she said. "You're a wonderful cook."

Like Brandon? He wanted to ask her, but knew it was better not to. He didn't want her making comparisons between him and her brother. That would quickly put him in the friend-zone. "This is only one meal."

"The best Johnny cakes I've ever had."

She didn't look as if she were pretending, she looked as happy as a child at Christmas. Even Dorothy hadn't fawned over his cooking like this. He almost wanted to cook more. He wanted to take out all the pots his brother had encouraged him to hide away and try a bunch of recipes on her.

She needed looking after. He'd managed to convince her to create snack packs to carry with her instead of living on energy bars. Maybe if he prepared and packed some good lunches...no. Lunches were a slippery slope. This breakfast would be it. A good memory. But soon she'd expect it and it wouldn't be special anymore. She'd roll her eyes and say "Johnny cakes again?" And he'd laugh and pretend that it didn't hurt that she wasn't impressed anymore.

"Sit down and eat some," she said.

"Only if you'll do something in return."

"What?"

"Marry me."

CHAPTER 39

Mindy stared at Trent open-mouthed. "Are you out of your mind? That wasn't part of the bet." They stood in the canned vegetable aisle of the global market. She'd asked for his help putting together a holiday dish she was to take to the office that week.

"I know."

She tugged on her large knit scarf. "I didn't think you'd take it this far and be so cruel. How are you going to break up with her?"

He picked up a can of tomatoes.

"Trent?"

He placed the can in the basket. "I'm not going to break up with her."

Mindy unraveled her scarf, balled it up then whacked him on the back of the head with it. "You can't *marry* her."

"Ow!" He glared at her. "Why not?"

"Because that would be a lie."

"No, it wouldn't. I want to marry her and she wants to marry me."

"She doesn't really know you."

"She knows me enough."

"I'm going to tell her."

"What are you going to tell her?" he asked, sounding bored as he strolled down the aisle. "And do you think she'll believe you when I tell her that I've changed?"

"You can't keep this up."

"I'll keep it up for as long as it takes."

"Trent—"

He turned to her, losing patience. "I'm not giving this up. Ever. Get used to it."

"Then you haven't proven anything except that you're still pathetic if you think it's okay to marry someone who doesn't truly love you."

He turned and went down another aisle, this one lined with spices. "She does love me."

"She loves a version of you you've made up. A façade. A mask. You'll be locked behind it for the rest of your life. You think that's love? You think that one day you won't resent her for it? How can you love someone you've been lying to? I bet you don't even know how you really feel about her except grateful that she's briefly made you forget your obsession with Dorothy."

Trent handed her the basket. "Then you don't know me at all."

But Mindy did know him and that was the problem. She knew about his past, his relationship with his family and how it had affected him, the true passion for his work. She also knew that he would start to resent Erin. He'd resent her for loving someone else, for loving a man who wasn't really him. He could pretend to be his brother and father, but the difference between him and them was how quickly they could move on. They never stayed alone for long.

But he would.

That was his future whether he was the old Trent or the new.

Erin had said yes to his proposal, light shining in her eyes and his heart had responded. He saw her as his bride; he pictured starting a family with her.

But he also remembered his parent's divorce. Would he want to bring a child into a relationship that was doomed? He'd proven what most women wanted. It was time to end the charade.

CHAPTER 40

He wasn't going to marry her.

Erin could tell by the look on Trent's face when she opened the door. She saw the regret. She tried to harden her heart against it, angered that she'd allowed herself to believe that his proposal was real. He shook his head when she gestured he come inside.

"I'm sorry," he said.

"You changed your mind."

He nodded.

She laughed without humor. "Somehow I thought it was too good to be true."

"I'm a fraud."

"What?"

"You were right when you said you felt I was holding something back from you. I was hiding who I really am and I'm sorry."

Okay. That wasn't so bad. She could handle that kind

of honesty. Her tension ebbed a little. "Will you give me a chance to find out who he is?"

"No."

She paused, shocked. "Why not?"

"I can't."

"Why not?"

"You still ask too many questions."

She rested her hands on her hips. "And I always will."

"All I can say is that I'm sorry and—"

Erin angrily yanked him inside and closed the door. "No, you can say a lot more than that. Why are you a fraud? Why did you lie? What did you lie about? Are you really Trent Brewster?" She waited then motioned for him to respond. "Are you?"

He nodded.

"Did you co-found SonTil Sounds?"

He folded his arms and nodded again.

"Were you in a bus crash at seventeen?"

"Yes, but—"

"And did you used to date Dorothy and loved her for two years until she found someone else?"

"Erin—"

"And do you have a cousin named Mindy who works at an animal shelter? Do you like Johnny cakes and sex with a woman?"

"You know I do, but I wasn't completely honest with you."

"Why? Why the act?"

"Act?"

She lowered her voice to mimic his. "No, I don't like

to cuddle. No, I'm not into talking." She returned her voice to normal. "I've dated so many jerks, I can spot them. No matter how you tried you were a nice guy and that's who I fell in love with. Did you know you hum the song "My Shot" from *Hamilton* when you're working on something? That you always cover me up when we're in bed to prevent me getting a chill? You never talk over me and you listen. You actually listen. Do you know how rare that is? You couldn't pretend to be a real selfish prick if you tried and I know you did. I stayed around for this moment. The moment when you'd give me the chance to love you as you truly are." She sighed. "But you're still too scared to. Scared I'll walk away."

"I know you will. You told me so."

"No I didn't."

"Yes, you did. You said 'I don't need another brother.'"

Erin rolled her eyes in frustration. "That's because I didn't want you to think you had to be whoever my brother wanted you to be. I didn't mean I didn't want you to be yourself. I was trying to make you feel better."

Trent shook his head. "No, you said it because it's the truth. You don't want someone hovering over you, worrying about you. You'd get bored of me."

"You don't know that." She softened her voice, her eyes pleading. "I want to find a way to make this work. I don't want to lose you. I've never met a guy like you. You're a great lover and you're like my best friend."

She might as well have slapped him. All his efforts to be the new and sexy Trent had been for nothing. That's how she saw him? A best friend? He could take anything but that.

Trent gripped his hand into a fist and gritted his teeth. "I don't want to be your damn best friend."

She looked at him startled. "Why not?"

"Because I'm ready to meet a woman who sees me as more than that. Who wants more than that. A woman who sees me as a man."

"But I didn't say—"

He opened the door.

"You're not a man," Erin spat out in a cold whisper.

Trent spun around not sure he'd heard her. His angry brown eyes met hers. "What did you say?"

She boldly stared back, contempt in her gaze. "You're. Not. A. Man. How can you expect any woman to see you as a real man when you're so cruel? You're a game player. An ass—"

He held up his hand. "Now wait a minute—"

"And I'm angrier at myself than I am with you," she said in a tight voice. "I hate that I let you fool me. I shouldn't have thought you had kind eyes and thought that meant you had a kind heart." She shook her head. "You're not kind. I always imagine people getting hurt in various ways, but never imagined you hurting me this much. You're dangerous like the bite of a poisonous reptile, a knife blade or a bullet and you leave scars deeper than the one on your neck. I'm sorry I ever met you."

CHAPTER 41

"The engagement's off," Trent said over the phone as he sat in his cold car, which was still parked outside Erin's apartment complex. Above him he saw holiday lights strung along several balconies tossing bright colors into the darkening sky while the echo of Erin's words continued to ring in his ears. *You're cruel. A poisonous snake. You leave scars. I'm sorry I ever met you.*

"What did you say?" Mindy asked.

"The engagement's off."

"No, what did you say to Erin? Was she upset?"

More than I can share. "Not really."

"I want details."

"I'm not giving details. Bye."

"Wait, wait. Don't go."

"Why not?" He shot back. "I'm not getting married, what more is there to say? I thought you'd be happy."

"I didn't want you to marry based on a lie."

He pounded the steering wheel. "It was real to me. And it could have worked if..." He sighed. "Doesn't matter. It's over now."

"Did you tell her why?"

"Why would I tell her about the bet?"

"Because she might understand if—"

"Right now she hates me and I feel the same."

Mindy's voice cracked in surprise. "You hate her? You've never hated anyone. You're upset. You don't mean it."

"I do because she—" He stopped. He didn't want to share that his strategy hadn't completely worked. That he'd fallen in love again and ended up in the friend-zone once more. He'd failed to get Erin to see him as her man. His heart hurt so much he thought it would burst. Trent briefly closed his eyes and steadied his breathing. He'd recover, he always did. He wouldn't make the same mistakes again. "All you need to know is that it's over."

BRANDON LOOKED AT ERIN CONFUSED. "BUT I DON'T understand."

She'd come to his apartment after Trent had gone and told him and Tara about her broken engagement. "What is there to understand?" Erin said. "He's a snake. I should have known when I met his brother. His father too."

Brandon shook his head. "No, he's not."

"You thought so when you first met him."

"I was wrong."

"You weren't wrong."

He rubbed his forehead. "This doesn't make any sense. I saw him...I saw him..."

"What?"

"Clean up your place."

"It was all an act," Erin said. "He was using me to get over Dorothy. That's all."

"I don't think—"

"You don't believe me? You're on his side?"

Brandon hesitated. "I'm not...I'm just confused."

"There's nothing to be confused about. I'm telling you who Trent really is. I messed up again. The men I like never like me in the same way. I thought he was different, but I can't choose men."

For the next hour Brandon let her vent while Tara plied her with sympathy and food. When she calmed down they said their goodbyes.

"What's that expression for?" Tara asked her husband once they were alone.

"They're good for each other."

"I know, unfortunately, they don't know it yet."

"And he loves her."

Tara sniffed. "You don't know that."

"I do," Brandon said adamant. "I saw it."

Tara paused. "What did you see?"

<hr>

Walks and work.

Work and walks.

That was all Trent could manage. He didn't want to

think about Erin. He'd done the right thing. He'd prefer having her angry at him than to see her grow tired of him. This was better. But he couldn't keep hating her, as much as he wanted to. And he couldn't forget her words either. He'd managed to get through almost a week without feeling numb. Perhaps in five years he'd start to feel human again.

Trent headed back home from a long walk with Roger when the brown Lab suddenly grew excited and started to tug on his lead. "We're almost home," Trent said confused. "What's the rush?"

He turned to his house and saw what had caught Roger's interest. Tara sat on the front step next to a pet carrier. She stood and smiled when she saw him. "Hi."

He walked up to her, his heart racing. Why was Erin's sister-in-law visiting him? Had something happened to Erin? He'd read about a local ER doctor who'd committed suicide. He knew the rates were high. Or was it a motorcycle accident? But Tara wouldn't have come over to tell him something like that and she certainly wouldn't have smiled at him if she had such awful news. Trent took a deep breath and said, as casual as he could manage, "What are you doing here?"

"I need a favor. Can we talk inside?"

Trent hesitated wanting to tell her 'no' before he said, "Sure."

Moments later they sat in his kitchen with cups of coffee, Sunny purring on his lap while Roger lapped up water in his bowl.

"What do you want?" Trent finally asked her.

"You have a very comfortable home."

Trent let his gaze drop and gritted his teeth. There was that damn word again comfortable. But he wouldn't run from it. That was who he was. He'd gotten rid of all the items that his brother had encouraged him to buy, donating them to a local Goodwill, and returned his house back to normal. So yes his house was comfortable, dull and boring. "Did Erin send you?"

"Why would she? She's seeing someone else."

His head snapped up and he stared at her, a bitter jealousy consuming him. Already? She'd gotten over him *already*? Someone else was hearing her laughter, feeling her touch? Someone else was with her? A wave of loneliness and despair nearly crushed him before he felt the stirrings of anger.

Of course she would move on. She hadn't really loved him in the first place. The women in his life always quickly found someone new. At least he wouldn't receive a wedding invitation.

Tara shook her head then said with a note of regret, "I'm sorry, I just needed to see if he was telling the truth."

"What? Who?"

"Brandon told me how you felt about Erin but I didn't believe him."

Trent frowned. "I don't understand."

"Erin's not seeing anyone."

She'd tricked him. Trent made sure his expression didn't change, although he hated the sense of relief he felt. "You said you needed a favor."

"Brandon and I want you and Erin to raise Sunny."

"That doesn't make any sense."

"Yes, it does. Look at her. She is happy with you and

she's the same way with Erin. It's not the same with us. She brought you two together once, let her do it again."

Trent placed Sunny on the ground. "It was merely a coincidence."

"So what?"

Sunny jumped back on his lap. He set her back on the ground again. Sunny made a sound of protest but Trent sent her a stern look so she did the equivalent of a cat shrug before she left the room to explore. He turned his attention back to Tara. "We're not together anymore."

"You're good for her. Erin has had a lot of bad luck with guys. She thought you were different."

"She was wrong."

Tara rested her chin in her hands and studied him. "No, she's not. You're not a coward. Those other guys who have lots of women, most of them are. They're afraid to risk their heart. To become attached to anyone. They don't know that it takes a brave man to risk heartbreak."

"She doesn't see me as a man."

"Yes, she does."

"No, she doesn't."

Tara opened her handbag and put a picture on the table. It showed her as a teenager lying in bed with a cast on her leg. "Guess how I broke my leg?"

He shrugged.

"Joy riding on a motorcycle, I shouldn't have been riding, in Italy." She laughed at his look of surprise. "I was a wild kid. Poor Brandon had to be there for me more times than I can count like when I broke my clavicle when I used to box. Or when I tore my Achilles running." She grinned and winked. "Even now I can keep him on his toes, although I'm more reckless in my stories than in real life. But he never got bored of me and I never got bored of him. If you don't want people to judge you, don't judge them. We're not all what we seem." She glanced at the fridge. "Give Erin a chance and tell her the truth."

"About what?"

Tara nodded to a picture of a baby surrounded by angels that was stuck on his fridge. "About her."

Trent felt his heart constrict. He'd taken the picture down in order to be the new Trent.

Tara's voice grew soft. "There's a story there, isn't it?"

He swallowed. He didn't talk about her or his sister Ana to anyone.

"And that pain needs to be shared with someone you love."

Trent shook his head. "She won't love me for it. She won't—"

"Why do you keep pushing away something that is already yours?" Tara nodded to his lap and he noticed that Sunny had returned and he'd been absently stroking her. "Go to Erin and tell her who you truly are. Let her see the man she loves."

"She doesn't love me."

Tara couldn't stop a smile. "Prove it."

He stood by her motorcycle. Trent was the last person Erin expected to see at the end of her shift. And she wanted to shout at him to leave her alone, but he looked cold and miserable.

"What are you—"

"My niece died. Her name was Maya. She was the inspiration for the idea of OnTheSpot. My sister, Ana, wanted to have a baby on her own and when she became pregnant I was so happy for her. I helped her decorate the baby's room. We're not a close family but she and I connected over her choice to do something outside of our family's expectations. It wasn't an easy pregnancy and despite her profession and money she wasn't always seen and treated as well as she could have been since she was a single, black woman. Once, on a trip out of town, she was left waiting in the ER for three hours, although she was showing signs of preeclampsia with swelling in her legs, fatigue, a headache and, later they discovered she also had high blood pressure.

"But everything was worth it when Maya finally came into the world and she was beautiful.

"Ana soon sensed something was wrong. Maya was crying almost all the time. Although Ana went to a number of doctors they dismissed Maya's symptoms as colic or gas or early teething. And our family—full of doctors—couldn't come up with anything because no one took the time to investigate. No one took the time to suspect what was truly the problem until it was too late. A twisted gut. It burst and killed her."

Erin covered her mouth in horror. "Trent, I'm so sorry."

"I cried for a year. Ana even longer. Maya was wanted and we loved her, but couldn't save her. Somehow, together we survived her loss. I never felt such pain and sense of helplessness so I turned to sound. I needed comfort. I'd grown up around hospitals but being there again made me angry. All the sounds and chaos. I had to do something productive. To make a change so that someone else wouldn't die due to neglect from an over-whelmed staff. I created OnTheSpot for her, and my niece gave me a reason to go on even though it couldn't have helped her directly.

"When I met you I still hated doctors. I grew up surrounded by their arrogance, egoism and greed. The Messiah complexes and megalomaniacs. I saw it in the way my sister was treated and dismissed. And Maya died because my family didn't care. They were too busy doing something else. They also never thought I was at their level because I chose a different field.

"I was angry for years and after Maya's passing I wanted to prove they were the fools. If only they'd listened. Nobody listened. So I turned to focusing on sound in hospitals. Despite the many failures. Despite my family's thoughts. And OnTheSpot failed many times. Until one day, it worked." He took a deep breath then said in a rush. "I've never told that story to anyone because I know how much it reveals about me. It shows I'm weak, I'm sentimental, I'm stubborn, I'm—"

"Wrong."

"What?"

"You're wrong." Erin looked around the parking lot. "Where did you park your car?"

"Why?"

"Because it's cold and you're going to treat me to something hot."

They didn't talk on the way to the local coffee shop or as they stood in line or even when they finally got a table. Erin let the silence stretch until Trent finally said, "What do you mean I'm wrong?"

Erin wrapped her cold fingers around the warm cup. "You don't know yourself. I've never met a man so clueless."

"And pathetic, right?"

"No. You're not that either. I think the true problem with you is that you listen too much and you believe what others say about you. I never would have made it to where I am today if I'd listened to what everyone said about me. You may feel pathetic sometimes but that doesn't make you pathetic, and crying is not a weakness. And loving a baby isn't being sentimental. Whoever told you so is wrong. I admire how much you love your sister. That's not a weakness either. You need to start listening to yourself. To your heart. To how you feel. You listen to everyone, but who listens to you? Why don't you demand that someone does? Because that's what you deserve."

Erin folded her arms. "And now you expect me to forgive you, right?"

He nodded.

"And if I don't?"

"I'll try to convince you how much Sunny needs a mother."

"And if that doesn't work?"

He pulled out his cell phone. "I'll play a song that I asked Vince to write and perform for you."

She frowned. "Vince?"

"Vince Tran. Heard you were a fan."

Her brows shot up. "You know him?"

Trent couldn't stop a grin. "He's a close friend."

Erin let her arms fall. She leaned forward and sent him a suspicious look. "What else haven't you told me?"

"How much I love you."

She narrowed her eyes, but a grin touched her lips. "Bastard."

"Am I forgiven?"

"Yes."

"Even though you said I was a poisonous reptile?"

"You were. You shouldn't have treated me like that."

"You said I was like your best friend," he said annoyed.

"I was wrong. You *are* my best friend."

"I don't want to be."

"Why not? I always wanted to marry my best friend."

Trent stared at her speechless. "*Marry* him?"

"Yes."

"Why?"

She winked. "I always thought it would be kind of sexy."

Sexy. Not comfortable, boring and dull. His heart began to pound and the light in her eyes made him know she wasn't teasing. "Really?"

She nodded. "I thought a lover and a best friend was a great two-in-one deal. But I wasn't sure I'd ever find a man like that." She held his gaze, and her voice softened, vulnerable. "Have I?"

Trent motioned her closer and gave her the only answer she needed.

ABOUT THE AUTHOR

Dara Girard, an award-winning, national bestselling author of more than forty books continues to gain readers with titles such as *Private Lessons, Always and Forever, Sweet Temptation,* and *Midnight Promise.* Dara loves to travel and hear from readers.

You can write her at:

contactdara@daragirard.com

or

P.O. Box 10345

Silver Spring, MD 20914

If you'd like to receive a reply, please send a self-addressed stamped envelope.

Visit her website to sign up for her newsletter and get sneak peeks, monthly updates on new releases, and special offers.

For more information visit
www.daragirard.com